"I don't [...]
you a [...]

"And to tell you the truth, I don't care," she went on. "There's only one point at issue, and that's your shocking lack of manners out there in the hotel foyer." She gestured toward the door. "And for which, incidentally, I'm still awaiting your abject apology."

For one hideous moment Oriel thought the man was going to have an apoplectic fit. His tall lean figure began visibly shaking with violent emotion, as a dark flush spread over his tanned features.

"I'm not in the habit of letting some uppity girl speak to me the way you did!" he said through clenched teeth, gripping her by the shoulders.

One moment she was falling backward, and the next, she felt herself being quickly grabbed, his arms closing about her slim figure to hold her in a tight embrace.

MARY LYONS is happily married to an Essex farmer, has two children and lives in an old Victorian rectory. Life is peaceful—unlike her earlier years when she worked as a radio announcer, reviewed books and even ran for parliament in a London dockland area. She still loves a little excitement and combines romance with action and suspense in her books whenever possible.

Books by Mary Lyons

HARLEQUIN PRESENTS

763—DANGEROUS STUNT
779—LOVE'S TANGLED WEB
796—MENDED ENGAGEMENT
828—ECLIPSE OF THE HEART
908—PASSIONATE DECEPTION
938—ESCAPE FROM THE HAREM
1002—HAY FEVER
1144—STRANGER AT WINTERFLOODS
1171—HURRICANE!
1276—LOVE IN A SPIN

Don't miss any of our special offers. Write to us at the following address for information on our newest releases.

Harlequin Reader Service
P.O. Box 1397, Buffalo, NY 14240
Canadian address: P.O. Box 603,
Fort Erie, Ont. L2A 5X3

MARY LYONS

no surrender

Harlequin Books

TORONTO • NEW YORK • LONDON
AMSTERDAM • PARIS • SYDNEY • HAMBURG
STOCKHOLM • ATHENS • TOKYO • MILAN

Harlequin Presents first edition March 1991
ISBN 0-373-11346-3

Original hardcover edition published in 1989
by Mills & Boon Limited

NO SURRENDER

CHAPTER ONE

JACOB WINTHROP EMMERSON III—a tall, dark and handsome, mega-rich banker of Boston, Massachusetts—was in a thoroughly pleasant, relaxed frame of mind as he wandered slowly through the busy, crowded bazaar in Aleppo.

Occasional white shafts of sunlight broke through the gaps in the high, vaulted roof of the ancient market-place, illuminating the fine leather saddles, camel-hair blankets and great sheepskin coats and carpets, all piled high and spilling forth in great profusion from the cluttered interiors of the many small shops and booths.

Currently leading a delegation from the International Monetary Fund, Jake was just congratulating himself on having managed to escape, both from his own financial advisers and the entourage of local Arab officials, when what he was increasingly coming to think of as a thoroughly evil, vindictive Nemesis—which had loomed over him throughout his business trip to Syria—unexpectedly materialised to strike him down yet again.

Standing at the entrance to a shop, he was admiring a large ebony screen heavily inlaid with mother-of-pearl when he was suddenly hit on the back by a hard blow, which sent his tall, broad-shouldered figure sprawling down on to a low pile of carpets.

Winded and gasping for breath, he didn't realise for a second or two that he was not, as he had at first supposed, lying trapped beneath a heavy bolt of cloth. It was impossible to see through the mass of loose brocade which lay across his face, but his exploring hands soon discovered that the object lying on top of him was warm, human and ... hmm ... yes—quite definitely female!

'Oh, lumme. I'm so sorry ...'

Jake stiffened, wild alarm bells ringing in his head as he registered the cool, clipped tones of an English accent.

'Hey!' The 'female' gave a muffled screech and began struggling violently. 'I don't know who you are ... but take your hands off me—at once! You—you disgusting brute!'

Gripped by a shocking presentiment, Jake's worst fears were quickly confirmed as he at last managed to free his arms and pulled aside the heavy length of material.

'Oh, no! I don't believe it—*not you again?*' he groaned, staring up at a cloud of rich golden hair, which surrounded the flushed cheeks and startling blue eyes lying above him.

Jake's two-week business trip to Syria had been carefully and meticulously planned. He had been exhaustively briefed by officials of the state department, and also the IMF—all of whom had assured him that they had taken care of every contingency. And yet what had happened? He had hardly arrived in this damned, fly-blown country before he had come slap-bang up against the fickle finger of malicious fate! *Why him*? That's what he wanted to know. What had he ever done to deserve the persistent, chaotic disruption of his life by this crazy English girl?

And the totally regrettable, not to say deeply irritating fact that he found Dr Oriel de Montfort *very* physically attractive only seemed to make matters worse, somehow. Heaven knows, he had always had the good sense to steer well clear of tall, bossy career women—however good-looking they might be. So how come that, within five minutes of first meeting this damned girl, he had had some sort of brainstorm . . . and kissed her? And why was it that every one of their subsequent ill-fated encounters had ended in *exactly* the same way?

Jake gave a heavy sigh, and tried to clear his normally crystal-clear mind. Unfortunately, it seemed as though the close proximity of Oriel's soft, warm body was having its usual disastrous effect on his ability to think clearly. Which was crazy—since nothing like this had ever happened to him in all his thirty-five years of calm, ordered existence. The only explanation that made any sort of sense was that he must be suffering from a case of temporary mental delirium. Because if there was one thing about which he had absolutely no doubts whatsoever, it was the need to keep a cool, clear head when in the vicinity of this quite insane female doctor.

And that was another thing: how she'd ever managed to get herself medically qualified was quite beyond him. She must be the kiss of death as far as her patients were concerned. *If*, of course, she had any patients left alive, which was something he very much doubted, he told himself grimly. Goodness knows, she'd nearly killed him in Palmyra—not to mention half drowning him in the pool at their hotel at Damascus. Oh, yes—this lady was trouble with a capital 'T', all right. In fact, if he managed to get back to the States in one piece it would be nothing less than a miracle!

Oriel gazed down into the cold, hard grey eyes, her heart sinking like a stone. From the very first day she had arrived in Syria, this man had persisted in suddenly appearing out of nowhere like . . . like some evil genie from a bottle. Heaven knows, she'd done her level best to keep out of his way, but wherever she went or whatever she did there he was—as large as life and twice as ugly!

Not that he was *really* ugly, of course. In fact, lying with a lock of his thick, dark hair falling over his hard-boned, tanned face, there was no doubt that the horrid man was extraordinarily good-looking; which had made his accusation that she was dogging his footsteps—the last time she had had the misfortune to see him—all the more infuriating. And why he should apparently think she regarded him as God's gift to women, she had absolutely *no* idea.

The plain truth was that, right from the first moment she had laid eyes on his tall, arrogant figure, striding through the hotel in Damascus as if he owned the place, she had instinctively hated his guts. Although that was something which the conceited oaf found impossible to believe, if his subsequent loutish behaviour had been anything to go by.

Quite apart from anything else, the man was obviously insane. Anyone who had the damned nerve to grab and kiss a complete stranger—only a few minutes after they had first met—was clearly a candidate for the funny farm. And when their subsequent meetings had ended up with her being firmly clasped in his arms, and he had had the brass nerve to accuse *her* of pursuing him . . . well, she'd had absolutely *no* doubt that Jake Emmerson was a raving lunatic! Surely, if he had an ounce of sense, he could see that it wasn't her fault they had kept—literally—bumping into one another.

Except—well, possibly . . . maybe . . . this time it was her fault. Not that she had tumbled into him deliberately, of course, but the large bale of cloth which she had pulled down from a high shelf in the shop next door had proved to be far more bulky and heavy than she had supposed. So much so that she had been in the very embarrassing position of finding herself staggering about like a Scotsman about to toss a caber. Unfortunately, as the material had begun to unravel, she hadn't been able to see where she was going.

So, it looked as if she would now have to apologise to the loathsome man. Goodness knows, the words would stick in her throat, but . . .

Oriel gave a sudden gasp, deep crimson flooding over her cheeks as she belatedly realised that the hands, which had been holding her so firmly, were now moving slowly and erotically over her soft curves. *Oh, heavens*! What on earth was she doing, lying here on top of him like this? She must be out of her mind!

Through nervous, fluttering eyelashes she saw that while she had been attempting to pull her distraught wits together the fiercely angry expression on his tanned face had subtly altered. The hard grey eyes were now conveying a message that was very different, causing her heart to begin pounding like a sledge-hammer as a fiery, heady streak of excitement spiralled through her body. Oh, no! Surely he wasn't going to kiss her—*not again*?

'I—er—I'm sorry . . .' she muttered, trying to release herself from the bale of cloth as she quickly wriggled sideways on to the pile of rugs. 'I mean, it's all been a most . . . a most unfortunate accident.'

'Oh, yes?' Jake gave a short bark of caustic

laughter. 'Heaven knows what I've done to deserve it, but will you kindly *stop* following me around this God-forsaken country?'

'I'm not!' she protested angrily.

'It sure looks like it to me,' he retorted grimly. 'There are approximately seventy-two thousand square miles in Syria, right? So, maybe you can tell me why it is that, wherever I go, the one thing I can be totally one hundred per cent sure of is that you are going to pop up, like some damned jack-in-the-box?'

Oriel's cheeks flamed, her slim form shaking with rage as she struggled wildly to escape from the loose folds of material.

'What arrogance!' She gave a high-pitched, scornful laugh. 'As far as I'm concerned, you are absolutely the *last* person I want to see. And, let me tell you, you pompous ass, that I——'

'Does madam wish to buy the cloth?'

The heavily accented Arab voice broke in upon them like a dash of cold water, causing Jake to quickly scramble to his feet and look about him in dismay.

'Oh, lord—that's all I need!' he groaned as he viewed the crowd of interested spectators gathering about the entrance to the shop. Swearing under his breath with impatience while Oriel brushed down her crumpled cotton skirt, he grabbed her arm as she was attempting to pin back the tendrils of hair which had escaped from the heavy coil at the base of her neck.

'Hey—what do you think you are doing?' she gasped. 'If you don't take your hands off me, I'll——'

'Shut up!' he growled, still keeping a firm grip on her arm as he turned to the shopkeeper. With a bland smile he pressed a large wad of banknotes into the Arab's hand before quickly striding off down the crowded alley-way, towing Oriel behind him.

'For heaven's sake, let me go!' she protested, finding that she was forced to run to keep up with his long stride. 'There's no need for this mad dash.'

He gave a snort of grim laughter. 'There's every need. Goodness knows what the Press would make of all that nonsense back there, but I need those sorts of headlines like a hole in the head! I'm not letting you out of my sight until I've deposited you back at your hotel. And maybe then—if I get *real* lucky!—I'll be able to relax.'

'But . . . but I don't want to go back to my hotel,' Oriel cried, trying to wriggle out of his grasp. 'I've still got some shopping to do.'

'That's just too bad,' he said ruthlessly as they left the noisy, crowded market, and emerged into the strong sunlight of one of Aleppo's main, tree-lined thoroughfares. 'OK, where are you staying?'

Grateful for the opportunity to get her breath back, Oriel stood glaring up at him with a mutinous expression on her face. Why should she let this foul man push her around? She still hadn't bought half the things she wanted to take home, and this souk in the northern city of Aleppo was famous for its silk brocade—just the thing for Aunt Harriet.

'Well?' he demanded.

'You're nothing but a . . . a rotten bully!'

'I can assure you that I am normally regarded as a very reasonable man,' he drawled. 'However, during the last two weeks—and certainly as far as any dealings with *you* are concerned—I've learned the necessity of cultivating a high level of self-preservation!' he added with a grim, sardonic bark of laughter. 'So let's stop wasting any more time. What's the name of your hotel?'

'I don't see why—*ouch!*' She winced as his fingers tightened on her arm. 'Oh—all right! If you must know, I'm staying at the Ramsis. But I'm not going to——'

'Oh, yes, you are!' he informed her bluntly as he signalled to a passing taxi. Bundling her into the vehicle, he gave the driver the name of the hotel before joining her in the cab.

I really, really hate him! Oriel told herself, inching as far away from his long-limbed figure as she possibly could. Staring glumly out of the window, she saw that they were passing the archaeological museum where she had spent some time yesterday admiring the ancient stone and bronze statues, many of which had been excavated by her father.

All her life, Oriel had hoped that some day, somehow, she would have the opportunity to get to know her father. However, that eccentric Frenchman, Professor Edouard de Montfort, had been so bound up with his archaeological 'digs' in the ruins of the great desert city of Palmyra that he had hardly been aware of her existence.

Actually, she reminded herself, she wasn't being entirely fair to her father. He had given her aunt plenty of money for his child's upkeep and education, but only seeing his daughter on the rare, brief occasions when he had happened to be visiting Oxford was hardly a basis for a father-daughter relationship.

There was no doubt that Edouard de Montfort should never have married. As Oriel's Aunt Harriet had so succinctly put it, 'The only women likely to interest your father had to be at least two thousand years old! Poor Ann never stood a chance.' But Ann Turnbull, a very quiet, shy girl—the complete antithesis of her forthright elder sister Harriet—had immediately fallen madly and hopelessly in love with the young French student who had come to stay with her father, Professor Turnbull, while furthering his archaeological studies at Oxford. Maybe it was because he found Ann's quiet personality to be very restful, or maybe—as her Aunt Harriet had suggested—the Frenchman had discovered that he rather liked being the object of silent worship and total adoration.

Whatever the reason, Edouard had almost absent-mindedly married the young girl, and equally carelessly had departed soon afterwards for the Middle East, quite forgetting to leave either a forwarding address or any mention of how or when he expected his new wife to join him.

'That was just typical of your father,' her aunt had told Oriel. 'A handsome, charming man—but existing on a different planet from the rest of us mortals. Mind you, right up to the day she died, my sister would never hear a word against your father, even though when he disappeared he must have known that she was expecting a baby.'

When Edouard had eventually returned to Oxford, it had been to find that his young wife had been killed by a drunken motorist while pushing a pram across a busy road. He had also discovered that he had a six-month-old daughter who had miraculously escaped unscathed from the accident. Taking it for granted that his wife's sister, Harriet, would continue looking after his child, he had instructed that she be called Oriel after his old college—and had swiftly departed abroad once more.

Gradually, over the years, her father's fame and reputation had become immense. Although she couldn't say she 'knew' him, Oriel was very proud of having such a distinguished father. He, for his part, on his very infrequent visits to

England, had been pleased to find that his daughter had inherited his academic ability, gaining a first-class degree in History, and then, two years later, her doctorate. If only he could have known that she was now a fellow of her college, and a lecturer in Medieval History. But three months ago Professor de Montfort had died of a sudden heart attack, and, although she was grateful for the Syrian Government's official invitation to visit his grave, Oriel dearly wished that she had some tangible, personal memories of her father to set beside his name written on the shiny brass plaques in Aleppo Museum——

'OK—out you get.' Jake Emmerson's voice cut abruptly into her thoughts, and she looked up to see that the taxi had drawn up outside her hotel. 'I can't say it's been a pleasure knowing you, Miss de Montfort, but it's certainly been an experience I won't forget in a hurry,' he said drily as he opened the door and helped her out of the vehicle.

'The feeling is entirely mutual!' she snapped, angrily brushing his hand aside. 'I can only hope and pray that I *never* have the misfortune of setting eyes on you again.'

'I'll second that!' He laughed. 'However, as I'm flying back to the States tomorrow, I guess we can both relax, hmm? So, I'll wish you *bon voyage*,' he added, giving her a sardonic bow before turning to stride off down the street.

'I hope your aeroplane falls out of the sky!'

she shouted after his tall figure, before quickly pulling herself together and stamping angrily up the steps of the hotel.

Crossing the foyer, she was just deciding to have a wash and brush-up before going back to the bazaar—she *definitely* wasn't prepared to have Jake Emmerson telling her what she could and couldn't do!—when she was hailed by the manager.

'Ah, the English meez.' He gave her a broad smile. 'I have a message for you—from the Minister of the Interior, *himself*,' he breathed reverently, bowing and scraping as he ushered her into his office.

'You must forgive me,' the manager continued. 'I had no idea . . . it has all been a most regrettable error. However, I have assured His Excellency that he need have no qualms—we have provided a veritable feast, and a car has been laid on to take you to the Meridian Hotel.'

'I don't think I quite understand,' Oriel muttered, glancing quickly down at her wrist-watch. Half the morning seemed to have gone already, and she was quite determined to finish her shopping—which had been so rudely interrupted!—before carrying on with her plan to visit Aleppo's ancient citadel this afternoon.

'Ah, dear lady. It seems the Minister, His Excellency Halim Khaddour, has heard of your need for transport back to Damascus. As he will be returning there himself today, I understand that he has kindly offered to take you with him in his limousine. I have been informed that a car will be arriving to collect you in half an hour, and I am happy to comply with the Minister's request to provide you with a luncheon to eat on the journey.'

'Oh . . . ah . . .' Bang go all my plans, thought Oriel, finding it difficult not to smile at the hotel manager's obsequious manner. He obviously expected her to practically swoon with delight at the thought of travelling with such an important member of the Government. And, in fact, good old Halim Khaddour's offer was a godsend. Travelling the three hundred miles back to Damascus in an air-conditioned limousine was certainly going to be far more comfortable than going by public transport—something she hadn't been looking forward to at all.

Flying from England to Syria via Paris, she had found herself sitting next to an American girl of her own age. Mary Lou, newly married to a Frenchman, had been delighted to meet her. 'It's so great to have someone to talk to—I still haven't got hold of the French language yet,' she'd said, and had introduced Oriel to her husband and the rest of their party of French archaeologists. They had, of course, all heard of her father, and had urged her to join their tour of the various classical sites and excavations. She had gratefully accepted their offer, and it had only been yesterday, when they had flown back to France from Aleppo, that she had begun to think about the problem of returning to Damascus.

Now, however, it seemed that her difficulty had been solved, and later, as she reclined in the luxurious vehicle which had been sent to collect her, she looked forward to an enjoyable trip. She certainly wasn't going to starve—not if that large hamper was anything to go by, she thought with a grin as the limousine drew up outside the hotel, which was set some way outside the city.

Warmly greeted by the Minister, she had no presentiment of the shock which fate held in store for her as he led her up the marble steps of the hotel.

Halim Khaddour was a small, plump, middle-aged man, whom she had never seen dressed in anything other than western-style clothes. An old friend of her father, he had been incredibly helpful in arranging her trip to Syria. The only slight fly in the ointment was that he did keep acting as if he had fallen for her like a ton of bricks. However, she comforted herself with the thought that maybe she was mistaken, and that his high-flown compliments meant nothing more than Arab politeness. In any case, there would be no problem in dealing with a man who, despite his elevated shoes, was at least a foot shorter than herself.

'I am *so* delighted to see you, my dear Oriel,' he was saying as he ushered her into the foyer of the hotel. 'These past few days have been

most exhausting! Of course, Syria needs the help
of the International Monetary Fund to develop
our hydro-electric schemes, but the eastern area
of my country is very barren, and not at all
picturesque. However,' he squeezed her hand,
'now that I can feast my eyes on your lovely
face . . .'

But Oriel wasn't listening to him. Her
horrified gaze was riveted on the tall,
broad-shouldered figure standing with his back
to her across the wide expanse of the marble
foyer. *Oh, no*! Surely it couldn't be . . .?

'Ah—here she is, Mr Emmerson,' Halim
Khaddour called out. 'Here is the lovely
"surprise" that I promised you! You see . . .?' He
turned to beam at the girl by his side. 'I knew
that this very important American gentleman
would be delighted to meet such a lovely lady.'

Oriel stared over at Jake Emmerson. Far from
being 'delighted', he was looking totally
stunned. It was as if a two-ton weight had just
dropped down from the sky, and
landed—*zonk*!—on top of his head. For a brief
moment he closed his eyes as a shudder ran
through his large frame. Then, taking a deep
breath, he began walking forward to where she
stood, rooted to the spot with shock and dismay.

'Ah, Mr Emmerson—can I have the pleasure
of introducing you to——?'

'There's no need for introductions, Minister,'
Jake drawled smoothly, although she noticed
that his hands were tightly clenched and a pulse

was beating wildly at his temple. 'I have already had the—er—pleasure of making this lady's acquaintance.'

'Yes—yes, we have met,' Oriel muttered grimly, making no attempt to match Jake's bland diplomacy.

Halim Khaddour seemed impervious to the chilly atmosphere between the two visitors to his country, who were glaring angrily at one another over his short figure.

'I have just spent two days with Mr Emmerson, showing him the Euphrates Dam at Al-Thaura, which has made such a dramatic difference to the irrigation problems we have suffered in the past. He tells me he was also very impressed with the other various hydro-electric projects which he has seen.'

Halim beamed up at Jake. 'Those kind words from such an important, international banker have indeed touched my heart,' the Minister added simply, raising his hand to his chest in a dramatic gesture.

'Yes—er—well . . .' Jake muttered, clearly not entirely comfortable with the Arabian tendency to indulge in over-elaborate, flowery compliments. 'However,' he added silkily, 'while I am, of course, delighted to meet Miss de Montfort again . . .'

That horrid man's ability to lie through his teeth is truly awesome! Oriel told herself, struggling against an overwhelming urge to kick him in the shins.

. . . nevertheless, Minister, if I am to see the oil refinery at Baniyàs, I do think we should be getting on our way.'

'Yes, of course, you are quite right,' Halim agreed, patting Oriel's hand. 'We have a long journey in front of us, and now—with such a charming companion—we shall enjoy it all the more, yes?'

Jake looked at him blankly. 'I don't think I quite understand? Are you saying that . . . that Miss de Montfort will be travelling with us?'

If she hadn't been feeling quite so angry with the man, Oriel would have found it difficult not to laugh at both the rising incredulity in his voice and the dawning horror which flickered across the American's hard, tanned features. The realisation that, despite having so rudely dumped Oriel back at her hotel, he was now still going to be forced to endure her company for the rest of the day was clearly making him feel as sick as a parrot!

And serve him right! Oriel thought grimly. She wasn't crazy about the idea, either. However, quickly deciding to make the best of an unfortunate situation, she gave Jake a broad, happy smile which she fervently hoped he would find extremely irritating.

'It's *so* kind of dear Mr Khaddour to give me a lift back to Damascus,' she said, in a soft, saccharin-sweet voice. 'And to actually have the honour of travelling with *such* an important man as yourself, Mr Emmerson—well!'

Oriel had to quickly turn her face away, desperately trying not to giggle at the dark, angry flush spreading over Jake's cheeks.

'Yes, I knew you would be delighted to have this dear lady's company on our trip,' Halim Khaddour said, blithely unaware that Jake's tall figure was rigid with fury. 'Miss de Montfort's father was one of my dearest friends,' Halim added, patting her hand again. 'His death was so sad. We are doing all we can to see that she has a pleasant stay in our country.'

'Um, yes, I'm sure you are,' Jake murmured, and Oriel flushed as she caught both the deep, sardonic note in his voice and the raised dark eyebrow with which he was cynically viewing her hand, now firmly held by that of the Minister.

'Ah, I see our new interpreter has arrived,' Halim said, waving to a group of people across the room. 'Alas, poor Abdul was taken ill in the night, but I am assured that his replacement, Miss Laila Saliman, is highly proficient.' He raised Oriel's hand briefly to his lips. 'I will just have a word with the other members of our party, and then we will be off, yes?'

Jake waited until the Minister was out of earshot. 'OK, little Miss Fix-it!' he snarled. 'I don't know what you think you're up to, but——'

'I'm not up to anything, you stupid man!' she hissed. 'The Minister offered me a lift—completely out of the blue—and when I accepted I had absolutely *no* idea that you came with the deal. Believe me, if I *had* known, I'd have turned the idea down flat.'

He gave a low, caustic laugh. 'Oh, yeah? Both you and Halim Khaddour looked pretty lovey-dovey to me!'

'You obviously have both a filthy mind, *and* a surprising lack of logic for someone who's supposed to be such a big cheese in the business world,' she retorted in a withering tone of voice.

'What the hell are you talking about?' he grated, pushing a hand roughly through his dark hair.

Oriel sighed. It was hot. She had been woken at the crack of dawn by an alarm call destined for another guest, and—above all—she was fed up to the back teeth with this tiresome man.

'All right, Mr Emmerson, let's take it from the top, shall we?' she grated. 'One—you apparently seem to assume—goodness knows why!—that I somehow craftily wormed my way into this trip, solely because I can't resist your fascinating personality! On the other hand, you also seem to think that I am romantically involved with the Minister. Now, you really can't have it both ways, can you?' she added, her voice heavy with sarcasm. 'QED . . . you are being thoroughly illogical.'

'Don't you lecture me, you . . . you dangerous harpy!'

'*Thank you*!' she was stung into retorting, until she realised that she had him intellectually on the run, and this was a perfect opportunity to give it to him—right between the eyes with both barrels.

'Item number two——' Oriel continued relentlessly, '—I was officially invited to this country to visit my father's grave. I am sure I don't have to tell you that travelling in Syria is difficult at the best of times, but a single woman faces insuperable difficulties. And my having an English passport doesn't help, either. Ever since the terrorist incident in London, Britain has severed diplomatic relations with Syria—which means that if anything goes wrong on this trip, I'm likely to find myself in a *very* dodgy situation.' She gave him a cold smile. 'With me so far?'

'Yes!' he snapped.

'OK—the third point logically follows, that, in order to get into this country and—hopefully!—get out again, I have needed all the help and protection I can find. So . . . far from being romantically interested in the Minister, or indeed you, Mr Emmerson—and, believe me, if I were *that* desperate, I'd shoot myself!—I am merely accepting a lift back to Damascus. Satisfied?'

With a face as black as thunder, he was prevented from replying by the approach of one of his assistants.

'The Minister is ready to leave now, sir,' the young man said, looking nervously at his boss and the pretty, slim blonde girl, who both seemed to be squaring up for a fight.

'I'll be ready in a moment!' Jake barked curtly.

'Yes, well, the thing is, sir—the Minister has decided that I, a couple of men from the Ministry, and the bodyguards will be travelling in the first car, which is leaving straight away. Apparently you, Miss de Montfort and the new interpreter will be travelling with the Minister in his limousine, which is not due to leave this hotel for another fifteen minutes.' The young man frowned and shook his head. 'I must tell you, Mr Emmerson, that I am not very happy about all the armed guards being in one car—nor the fact that the two limousines will be travelling so far apart.'

Jake shrugged. 'I don't see that there is any problem.'

'Well, sir,' his aide persisted, 'I picked up some rumours, and it appears that all the top guys in the Government have been warned to keep a wary eye out for various terrorist factions, and——'

'The internal politics of this country have nothing to do with me,' Jake told him firmly. 'This is strictly business, and, since the Minister is organising our trip, I suggest that we had better just leave everything to him.'

Oriel was left in absolutely no doubt, from the hard, icy glare he cast in her direction, that given half a chance he would boot her out of the Minister's car and go on his way, rejoicing.

Still—what did she care? Thanks to her father's old friendship with Halim Khaddour she would be travelling back to Damascus in considerable style and comfort. And if that male chauvinist American banker, Jake Winthrop Emmerson III, didn't like it . . .? Well, as far as she was concerned—that was just too bad!

CHAPTER TWO

ORIEL gazed out of the window as the
limousine left the motorway and began
climbing up into the foothills of the Jebel el
Ansáríye, the jagged but continuous mountain
range which divided the Syrian desert from the
country's lush Mediterranean coastline.

It certainly made a change from the
monotonously flat, arid, treeless landscape
through which they had been travelling for the
past hour, and Oriel was looking forward to
what the Minister had promised would be 'a
delightful al fresco experience'. She smiled to
herself as she realised that Halim Khaddour was
obviously unused to picnics, although he was
certainly in his usual top form as far as his
response to women was concerned. In fact, he
seemed to have been totally bowled over by his
new interpreter.

There was no doubt that Laila Saliman was
beautiful. Although Oriel, after a quick sideways
glance at the girl sitting next to her, had to admit
that the description was woefully inadequate.
With long dark curly hair framing a translucent
complexion which most film stars would have
given their eye-teeth for, huge black eyes fringed
with the longest eyelashes she had ever seen,

28

and a perfect nose set over soft red lips—Laila wasn't just beautiful, she was absolutely stunning!

And that wasn't all, Oriel thought gloomily. The Arab girl's perfect, hour-glass figure was poured into a short-sleeved bright red linen dress, whose demure high neck only seemed to emphasise her tiny waist and perfect bosom. On top of which, it looked as if Laila's fairy godmother, not content with bestowing such perfection on the girl, had become totally carried away—because she also appeared to be extremely bright and intelligent.

It was all *too much*—and Oriel found herself harbouring deep, dark thoughts of which she knew she ought to be thoroughly ashamed. But, really! While she might expect Halim to be almost ecstatic about Laila, it was absolutely pathetic to note the way Jake Emmerson was reacting to the new interpreter. He was looking completely stunned, as if he had never set eyes on anyone quite so ravishing in all his life. Which, after all, wasn't surprising, Oriel quickly told herself, glumly ashamed of her own sour reaction to the beautiful girl sitting beside her. Because, to tell the honest truth, neither had she.

Unfortunately, the interior of the luxuriously fitted limousine had been constructed in such a way that she and Laila were sitting on two 'chairs', which folded out to face the occupants of the rear bench-seat. So, she was finding it practically impossible to avoid seeing the way in which Jake and Halim were responding to the other girl's charms.

Maybe she wouldn't be feeling quite so depressed if she hadn't made a serious error when packing her suitcase for the trip. Oriel had automatically assumed that the pale cotton prints, so charming beneath an English summer sky, would be equally suitable for this country. Unfortunately, she had soon discovered that, in the strong, brilliant sunlight of Syria, her clothes appeared to be merely drab and boring. And lecturing herself, today, on the evils of female vanity had proved to be of *no* consolation whatsoever.

There was nothing wrong with her blouse and matching full skirt, in a Laura Ashley print of pale blue flowers on a sand-coloured background. In fact, it was a very practical choice for travelling in a hot, dusty climate. But Oriel was quite certain that even a saint, if forced to sit beside Laila Saliman, would have found it hard not to feel thoroughly dejected. It was like . . . well, like putting a dingy sparrow next to a brilliantly coloured bird of paradise!

Oriel sighed and leaned back in her seat. She was merely travelling in this car because it was the quickest and easiest way of getting back to Damascus. There was absolutely no point in allowing herself to become depressed by the startling contrast between herself and the Arab girl, she told herself firmly, closing her eyes and trying her best to ignore the surrounding buzz of conversation and laughter.

What did she care if Jake wanted to make a fool of himself? That was his business, wasn't it? The American might be a distinguished international banker with a family pedigree as long as his arm, but *she* wasn't impressed. Not like Mary Lou, who had positively drooled when, two weeks ago, Jake had marched through the foyer of the hotel in Damascus.

Oriel's lips tightened as she recalled her first sight of the man whose appearance had cast such a long, menacing shadow over her visit to Syria . . .

'Isn't he fantastic?' Mary Lou had whispered, giving Oriel a quick dig in the ribs.

'Who . . .?' Oriel muttered, not really listening to what the American girl was saying as she concentrated on filling in the hotel registration form. It had been a long flight from Paris, and, after listening to Mary Lou's non-stop chatter for over four and a half hours, Oriel was feeling not only travel-weary but also mentally exhausted.

'I love my Pierre, of course, but I really go for that lean, hard type of guy. How about you, honey?'

Oriel sighed as she received another sharp dig in the ribs, and, putting down her pen, she turned to see what Mary Lou was getting so excited about.

'*Him*!' the American girl hissed out of the corner of her mouth as the tall figure of a man, accompanied by several young men carrying bulging briefcases, bore down upon them.

'The key for my suite,' the man demanded in a clipped American accent.

It had been a long, tiring day, and Oriel was not prepared to put up with any nonsense. '*I* am being served at the moment,' she said firmly. 'So, I'd be grateful if you would kindly wait your turn.'

The tall stranger took no notice, continuing to ignore her existence as he once again demanded his key, impatiently snapping his fingers at the receptionist . . .

Thinking about it afterwards, Oriel was completely unable to account for what had happened next. She could only suppose that she had been suffering from a severe case of jet lag, which, combined with her sense of outrage at the man's rude behaviour, had resulted in her losing all control of her temper . . .

'Hey—you!' she shouted, raising her arm and swatting the man on the shoulder with her rolled-up newspaper.

There was a sudden hush in the large marble foyer of the hotel, all the bystanders seeming to hold their breath as the tall figure stiffened, before very slowly turning around to face her.

'I beg your pardon?' His voice was icy cold, his eyes hard grey chips of granite as they swept dismissively over the girl standing beside him. 'Were you, by any chance, speaking to me?'

'I most certainly was!' Oriel snapped, her fury

and resentment deepening at his obvious contempt for her dishevelled appearance.

So, OK—maybe her grey linen suit was looking a bit crumpled and creased from the long journey; and maybe she would have looked a lot better if she had been able to repair her make-up and to tidy her long pale gold hair, tendrils of which kept escaping from the heavy coil at the nape of her neck. But that was no excuse for him to be regarding her as though he had just discovered something nasty in the woodshed!

'And just *what* did you wish to say?' he enquired in a hard, patronising tone which set her teeth on edge.

'I wish to say—that it is quite evident that you are no gentleman!' she retorted, noting with grim satisfaction the fierce clenching of his jaw as her high, clear voice echoed around the hushed foyer. 'It must be obvious, even to a blind man, that I was in the process of being served by the receptionist.' She gestured towards the young Arab, who was now looking distinctly nervous and apprehensive. 'I certainly don't expect to be elbowed out of the way——'

'I did nothing of the kind!' he grated angrily.

'—by a boorish oaf with no manners!'

'By a—*what*?'

With the man's bellow of rage ringing in her ears, Oriel began to suspect that she might have gone too far. A quick glance around at the shell-shocked faces of the other hotel guests only served to confirm her worst fears.

Just as she was beginning to wonder how best to extricate herself from the unpleasant scene, she found her arm suddenly gripped by fingers that bit into her flesh like fierce talons. And before she knew what was happening, she found herself being quickly dragged away, into a room which lay behind the reception desk.

'*Out*!' the tall stranger barked at the occupants of the small office, who were clearly only too happy to obey his command. They scuttled from the room and he slammed the door loudly behind them.

There was a long silence as the two protagonists stared at one another. Eventually, the man gave an exasperated sigh, roughly pushing a hand through his dark hair as he began pacing up and down the room.

'Look, I don't know who the hell you are. But I've had a long, hard day at the Finance Ministry, and I don't need——

'Well, that's just too bad!' she interrupted angrily. 'Because I've had a long, hard flight from Paris, and *I* don't need someone being so rude to me in public!'

'I can assure you that I am not in the habit of losing my temper,' he informed her grimly. 'And certainly not in public.'

She gave a shrill laugh. 'You could have fooled me!'

'I'm also not in the habit of letting some uppity girl speak to me as you did!' he added through clenched teeth.

'Really?' Oriel muttered, trying to calculate the distance between herself and the door, and not assessing her chances of escape too highly.

'Yes, really!' he growled, pausing to glare at her with acute dislike.

'Well, that's of no interest to me,' she retorted. 'I don't know who you are—and, to tell you the truth, I don't care. It wouldn't make a scrap of difference to me, even if you turned out to be the President of the United States himself. There's only one point at issue, and that's your shocking lack of manners out there in the hotel foyer.' She gestured towards the door. 'And for which, incidentally, I'm still waiting to hear your abject apology.'

For one hideous moment, Oriel thought the man was going to have an apoplectic fit. His tall, lean figure began visibly shaking with violent emotion as a dark flush spread over his tanned features. She could have sworn that she actually heard his teeth being furiously ground together.

'Now, calm down—there's no need to get too excited,' she muttered nervously. She didn't care for the strangled sounds of rage issuing from his throat, nor the way his large hands were clenched so fiercely together, as if twisting rope—or possibly her neck . . .? 'I'm sure you must have had a reason for being so rude,' she added, hurriedly backing away as he advanced threateningly towards her.

'If I didn't, I sure as hell have one now!' he hissed menacingly. 'What are you—some nutcase let out of an asylum?' he demanded, gripping her fiercely by the shoulders and shaking her like a rag doll.

'I . . . I'm Dr Oriel de Montfort, and leave me alone, you . . . you brute!' she gasped, wincing as his vicelike grip tightened. 'If you don't stop, I'll call the police, and—*aagh*!'

Because he was so much taller and heavier than she was, the man's angry momentum had pushed her struggling figure backwards, their progress suddenly halted as she stumbled over a heavy, metal waste-paper basket. One moment she was falling backwards, and then, a second later, she felt herself being quickly grabbed, his arms closing about her slim figure to hold her in a tight embrace.

There was a long silence as they gazed at each other in shocked surprise. She was aware of a pulse beating furiously at his temple, the glittering cold ice of his stormy grey eyes, and the dark, angry flush beneath his tanned cheeks; and then she felt his arms tightening involuntarily about her slim, soft figure.

'*No!*' she managed to gasp, before he swiftly lowered his dark head.

It was an angry, savage kiss. The lips so ruthlessly possessing her own became a fierce, cruel instrument of torture that seemed to ravage her senses. And then . . .? Well, goodness knows how it happened—but it certainly wasn't her fault. Frantically beating her fists against his broad chest as she fought and struggled to escape his iron grip, she couldn't have said when the scorching pressure of his mouth eased and took on a persuasive quality. All she did know was that, by the time she realised what was happening, she had—somehow—lost all will to resist the lips moving so erotically over her own.

Oriel would have *died* rather than admit the dreadful truth. But, almost of its own volition, her traitorous body began to respond, melting helplessly against his hard frame as if drawn by some magnetic force totally beyond her control. Warmth and excitement ran like quicksilver through her veins as his kiss deepened and his hands began moving slowly over her soft curves . . .

Heaven knows where it would have all ended! Luckily she had been saved—if not exactly from a fate worse than death, than from something very much like it—by a loud cough. And, even then, it had taken them both some time to realise that they were no longer alone.

With an abrupt movement, she had found herself released as he had stepped sharply back, cursing violently under his breath and running his hands distractedly through his dark hair. Dazed and trembling, Oriel had slowly begun to focus, her horrified gaze following Jake's towards where a group of people were standing in the open doorway.

Even now, just thinking about the unfortunate episode was enough to make her go hot and cold all over. At the time, she would have given *anything* for a large hole to have opened up at her feet. She simply couldn't remember how she had got herself out of the room. Her only impressions were those of the receptionist's cheeky grin, the fawning attitude of the hotel manager towards the hateful man who had just assaulted her, and the sight of Mary Lou's mouth, hanging open wide with astonishment. And, of course, it was Mary Lou—even if she had meant well—who hadn't been able to resist rubbing salt in Oriel's wounds.

'Wow-wee, honey—that was some clinch!' the American girl had giggled, after knocking on Oriel's bedroom door to see if she was ready to go down for the evening meal. 'You do know who that guy was, don't you?'

'No, I don't know—and, frankly, I couldn't care less!' Oriel had said curtly. 'And I've decided to eat in my room tonight,' she'd added, shuddering at the thought of having to face the hotel staff and guests, most of whom had witnessed the deeply embarrassing scene downstairs in the hotel foyer.

'Well, honey, that was Jake Winthrop Emmerson III!' the unstoppable Mary Lou had continued blithely. 'I mean, he just happens to be one of *the* richest men in America—and a regular Boston brahmin, if you know what I mean.'

'I have no idea what you're talking about,' Oriel had muttered, furiously dragging clothes from her suitcase. 'But I don't care if he is God Almighty—he's still a thoroughly nasty, bad-mannered, male chauvinist pig!'

Mary Lou had gazed at her with startled eyes. 'But I thought——'

'You thought—what?' Oriel demanded aggressively.

'Well, you two did seem very . . . I mean to say, it's perfectly understandable, seeing as how he's such a gorgeous man and all . . .' She paused hopefully, but, when Oriel's only response was a muffled groan of fury, she quickly changed tack, obviously anxious to impress upon her new friend the worldly importance of the horrid man.

'You don't seem to understand. That guy's not only as rich as all get-out, and something really big in the IMF, but his family practically wrote the social register, for heaven's sake! His wife, too, came from one of the oldest——'

'I might have known he was married,' Oriel said scornfully. 'And, as far as I'm concerned, that only makes his behaviour even *more* disgusting!'

'No, no.' The American girl shook her head. 'He *was* married, but his wife ran away years ago with—oh, what's his name? You know . . . that famous Argentinian polo player . . .?' She clicked her fingers impatiently as she tried to recall the name.

'Serve him right! I wouldn't stay five minutes

with him myself.'

Mary Lou laughed. 'Well, I can tell you that thousands of women would, honey! I mean, he's definitely at the top of every red-blooded American girl's shopping list, *and* he can trace his ancestors right back to the Mayflower,' she added, her voice heavy with awe. 'My folks live in Boston, so I know what I'm talking about.'

'Oh, pooh! Who cares about that sort of nonsense?' Oriel had given a snort of derision. 'Anyway,' she had continued as the other girl had gazed at her with shocked, incredulous eyes, 'I'd be grateful if you'd drop the subject, especially as I'm never likely to see the awful man again.'

Talk about famous last words! Oriel's face flamed as she recalled all her subsequent, highly embarrassing encounters with the 'awful man'.

'Miss de Montfort . . .? Are you feeling all right?'

Halim Khaddour's voice broke through her confused thoughts, and Oriel opened her eyes to find both men staring at her.

'You seem very flushed,' the Minister added, gazing at her with concern.

'I'm fine, I . . .' Her voice died away as she caught the sardonic gleam of amusement in Jake Emmerson's grey eyes. He couldn't possibly have read her mind, could he? She felt quite sick for a moment before she realised that, no, of course he couldn't. All the same . . . I really, *really* hate that man, she thought viciously, seized by a childish longing to kick the shins of those long, elegantly clad legs within striking distance of her own.

Oh, lord! Just look at the effect he was having on her, for heaven's sake! All her life she'd prided herself on being a cool, calm, unruffled sort of person, and yet—within a space of two short weeks—she was now in imminent danger of turning into a mean and nasty, bad-tempered virago.

Oriel was still lecturing herself on the virtues of attempting to remain serene and unflustered, despite any provocation from Jake, when the vehicle slowed down in front of a large white sign before taking a sharp left-hand turn up a narrow road.

The Minister gave an exclamation of annoyance, pressing a button to lower the glass which separated the occupants of the car from the chauffeur in front. There was a rapid exchange of Arabic before Halim sighed and raised the glass again.

'My chauffeur tells me that this diversion is necessary because of repairs to the main road,' Halim explained. 'We shall, undoubtedly, return to the main route very soon. However, Miss de Montfort looked a little flushed just now. Maybe we should stop and have a breath of fresh air, yes?'

'Oh, I'm sure there's no need for such drastic measures, Minister,' Laila said quickly, giving Oriel no time to reply. 'Possibly just opening one of the windows would be the answer—wouldn't you agree, Mr Emmerson . . .?' she added, throwing him a wide, beaming smile.

There's no need to overdo the charm, sweetie! Oriel told her silently, seething at being so conspicuously ignored by the other girl. However, her glum thoughts were interrupted as Halim suggested that it might be about time they thought of stopping for their picnic.

'Well, actually——' Oriel began, not wanting to sound too greedy—even if she was feeling hungry enough to eat a horse. However, before she could say any more Laila had quickly intervened once more.

'But, dear Minister, this rugged terrain is so beautiful,' the Arab girl said with an enchanting, hesitant smile. 'I'm sure the English lady is in no hurry for her meal. Surely she would prefer to continue enjoying the passing scenery?'

No, I wouldn't! Oriel thought, casting a bitter glance at Laila. Her bad temper was not improved by catching sight of Jake's wide, cynical grin. It was clear that not only did he realise that Oriel was exceedingly hungry, but that he was also enjoying her discomfiture.

Why shouldn't I just come right out and say that I'm starving? Oriel asked herself. And she was just about to do so when she was yet again frustrated by Laila, who suddenly began pointing excitedly out of the window.

'What is that quite extraordinary structure?' she cried.

'Ah, yes. I haven't seen it before, but I think

. . . yes, I think it must be our exciting new discovery.' Halim beamed at them. 'It's a very old crusader castle, and until two years ago no one knew it was there. Of course, we have many such castles lining this mountainous coast—Krak des Chevaliers, near Homs, being the most famous,' he explained to Jake.

Oriel twisted around in her seat, her hunger forgotten as she stared up at the large stone structure perched like an eagle's nest high on a crag above them.

She had been saving her proposed visit to Krak des Chevaliers—the Castle of the Knights—and the other crusader castles lining the western strip of the Syrian coast, until the end of her visit. Apart from her obvious wish to visit her father's grave, it was the main reason why she had persisted against such tough odds to obtain a visa to visit the country.

For the past year, most of her spare time had been spent writing what, she hoped, would be the definitive book on medieval warfare. Now it was almost finished, and she had a publisher interested in the project, she felt that it was essential to personally explore the sites where, in the eleventh and twelfth centuries, the crusading knights from Europe had built their great defensive castles against the Saracens.

'Ah, yes, it is a truly magnificent sight,' Halim was saying as the road curved around the high mountain peak. 'But, up to a few years ago, there were so many trees and shrubs growing on the walls that it was completely hidden from view.'

'How did anyone, let alone knights on horseback, get up there?' Jake asked, gazing up at the ancient stone walls of the castle rising above the steep mountainside.

Oriel, who had been just about to ask the same question, gave him a grudging look of approval.

'You are right—it was difficult,' Halim agreed. 'Even when the castle was discovered, it proved impossible to cross the deep ravine in front of the entrance. It was only when a temporary metal bridge was thrown over the wide gap that it was possible to enter the castle.'

'I don't see any bridge,' Jake muttered, staring intently out of the windows.

Halim chuckled. 'That is because the castle has a sheer mountain drop on three sides. However, I am told that there is a track off this road which leads up to the entrance on the other side of the mountain.'

'It must have taken some building,' Jake said slowly, eyeing the massive slabs of stone which comprised the castle walls. 'Although it looks in pretty good shape to me.'

Halim nodded. 'Yes, for the past two years restoration has been carried out, and even a small museum was planned. However, work has now ceased for the time being, since it proved to be far too inaccessible for most tourists. Although I think——'

'Ah, look, Minister—that seems a perfect

place for our picnic!' Laila exclaimed,
apparently changing her mind as she pointed to
what appeared to be a lay-by on the other side
of the road, beneath the castle. Although the
unexpectedly flat piece of ground was covered
with massive rocky boulders, there was still
clearly room in which to park the car.

Halim quickly issued instructions to the
chauffeur, and the vehicle slowed down and
drove off the road on to the rocky surface.

'You are quite right. This seems a perfect
place for our picnic,' the Minister told Laila as
he opened the door, allowing the Arab girl to
descend before following her out of the limousine. 'I am sure that we would all like to . . .'
Halim's cheeks flushed with embarrassment.
'We—er—the ladies . . . the opportunity to re-
lieve ourselves . . .' he mumbled. 'I suggest that
we all meet back here in, say, five minutes?' he
added quickly before walking round to have a
word with the chauffeur.

'After you,' Jake said, opening the door on
their side of the vehicle, and giving an impatient
sigh as Oriel struggled with the collapsible seat.

'I can't seem to get it to work . . .' she muttered,
and when he gave another loud sigh of irritation
she became so fed up with the contraption—and
Jake—that she bent down, fiercely grabbing at a
handle beneath the chair. A brief second later it
came away in her hand, and Oriel found herself
tumbling forward on to the rear seat—and into
Jake's arms.

CHAPTER THREE

'THE dreaded "de Montfort Curse" strikes yet again, I see!' Jake drawled.

Oriel shook her head, still feeling shocked and dazed at finding herself so unexpectedly propelled into his arms. 'I don't know what you're talking about,' she muttered, trying to pull herself together to face yet another of his acid comments. However, to her astonishment, he merely gave a light laugh as he removed the broken handle of the seat from her hand.

'Oh, no?' he murmured, raising a sardonic eyebrow. 'I reckon that the "Curse of King Tutankhamun's Tomb" has nothing on the jinx which you carry around with you, Oriel!'

'That's ridiculous! I——'

'Yup, you've got the evil eye, all right!' he added with a wry laugh. 'Half drowning me in that pool in Damascus was a perfect illustration of the sort of hex you cast over other people's lives.'

'That's totally unfair!' she protested, glaring at him with dislike. How could she have known that he wasn't drowning when she'd 'rescued' him from the hotel pool in Damascus, only three days after she had first arrived in the country? Anyone could have made the same

46

mistake. After all . . . when you saw a body floating head down in a swimming-pool, it was perfectly natural to assume that the worst had happened. In that sort of emergency, you didn't stop to think about the various possibilities—you acted! As for his subsequent explanation—that he was studying the antique tiles which had been used to line the bottom of the pool—well, that crazy idea would *never* have occurred to her—not in a million years!

As so she'd told him when, after having been obliged to use *considerable* force, she had eventually managed to drag his heavy body to the side of the pool.

Unfortunately, Jake hadn't been at all appreciative of her efforts to save his life. 'My life wasn't in danger—not until you came along!' he had roared angrily, nursing his bruised jaw and swearing loudly about 'stupid **** women who didn't mind their own **** business'.

Not only had Jake's language been *thoroughly* disgusting, but he had also demonstrated his total lack of manners by savagely clasping her in his arms, possessing her lips in a fierce, angry kiss—and then roughly tossing her back into the water.

This man wasn't just horrid, he was a total barbarian! she now told herself, scowling up into his handsome face. 'I've already apologised about the unfortunate episode in the swimming-pool,' she muttered crossly. 'I mean—that sort of mistake could happen to anyone, couldn't it?'

Jake gave a harsh bark of laughter. 'One mistake—maybe. But how many times have you caused me grievous bodily harm, huh? What about that little "mistake" at Palmyra?'

'That wasn't my fault. How was I to know you were standing by the pillar?' she grumbled.

And it really *hadn't* been her fault. The visit to the ruined, desert city of Palmyra had been one of the high spots of her trip. All she'd been doing, that unfortunate day, was trying to take some photographs of the Great Colonnade at sunset. It would have made a marvellous picture—the thirty-foot-high pillars stretched for nearly a mile—and it was one she had been determined to capture on film before she went home. What was wrong with that?

'I realise that it is probably a waste of time,' Jake gave her an ironic half-smile, 'but most people do actually look where they are going!'

'I do—well, most of the time, anyway,' she amended quickly as he gave a grunt of cynical laughter. The trouble was, she had been trying to get as much into her photograph as possible, and she hadn't realised as she moved backwards across the sand that there were yet more pillars behind her. Not until, that is, she had abruptly collided with one and had ricocheted sideways, bumping into a tall figure who had been standing by the edge of a deep archaeological trench.

'I wish you'd stop going on about that episode

in Palmyra,' Oriel muttered gloomily. 'I've already said that I'm sorry—I don't know how many times.'

And she was sorry—she *definitely* was. Quite apart from bumping into his tall figure—the result of which had been to push him smartly down into the deep trench—she'd fallen in, too, hadn't she? And, although she had been lucky to break her fall by landing on top of Jake . . . he, unfortunately, had not viewed her sudden descent in *quite* the same way.

Her cheeks flushed as she recalled his extremely angry reaction, the hard pressure of his long body against hers as their limbs had become entangled, and the fury as he swore violently under his breath, rolling her over on to her back and proceeding to roughly possess her lips in a kiss of devastating intensity, the like of which she had never known before.

'You know what?' Jake's mocking voice cut into her distraught thoughts. 'I was almost certain that you were a natural disaster on two legs, but now . . .' he held up the broken handle of the car seat ' . . . now, I'm totally convinced of the fact!'

'Ha, ha!' she muttered bitterly, preoccupied with trying to sit up and, at the same time, to push her blouse, which had somehow come adrift, back under the waistband of her skirt. 'Anyway,' she added with a shrug, 'it's hardly my fault that part of this car has metal fatigue, is it?'

'Oh, I don't know . . .?' he mused, staring up at the roof of the limousine. 'I seem to suffer from *mental* fatigue whenever you're anywhere near me—so who's to say that iron and steel don't feel the same way about you?' he asked, before giving her such a wide, infectious grin that she was unable to prevent herself from smiling back at him.

'Now, that's a definite improvement!' he mocked softly. 'It's a pity for such a beautiful girl to be ranting and raving all the time.'

'Now, just a minute!' she snapped, her brief spell of good humour quickly fading away. 'I hope you aren't having the nerve to accuse *me* of ranting and raving.'

'Heaven forbid!' he murmured piously.

Oriel gazed up at the tanned face, only inches away from her own. She was perfectly well aware that the horrid man was laughing at her—she would have to be blind not to see the glinting amusement in those grey eyes now staring down at her so intently. But she was tired of arguing every point with him. For one thing, it was far too hot—and for another . . . for another . . .

It suddenly seemed to require an enormous amount of effort to force her brain to think constructively—about anything. She was mesmerised by the strange gleam in his eyes, only conscious of the musky scent of his cologne, and the hard strength of the arms holding her close to his warm body. Close to his—*what*?

Oriel came to her senses with a bang, a deep tide of crimson racing over her face as she realised that she was still lying in his arms. And what had happened, every time that she had found herself in that selfsame situation . . . and particularly in Palmyra? *Oh, no!* She wasn't going to let herself think about the way he'd kissed her . . . *No, she wasn't!*

'I must get out of here!' she cried, frantically trying to wriggle out of his embrace.

Jake gave a rueful laugh. 'What's your hurry?' he drawled sardonically. 'Every time we've met, you've ended up in my arms. So, what's different about today, hmm?'

'Nothing—I mean—everything! Let me go!' she wailed, finally managing to scramble out of the car. Running away across the dusty ground, his caustic peals of laughter echoing in her ears, she took shelter behind some large boulders.

Leaning her back against the warm rockface of a boulder which was twice her height, Oriel's hands trembled as she took her handkerchief from her pocket and mopped her brow. What was happening to her, for heaven's sake? Her heart was thudding like a tom-tom, and she was so out of breath from that short run that possibly she ought to see a doctor?

She'd been one hundred per cent fit all her life, but maybe she *did* have some terrible disease—a brain tumour, perhaps?—because she was totally unable to account for the quite extraordinary, peculiar way in which her sense of time had suddenly gone so awry. Ever since she had arrived in Syria, and whenever she found herself alone with Jake, it seemed to Oriel as though all the clocks in the world immediately stopped ticking; as if, somehow, time and space had no meaning. And that really was crazy, because she didn't even like the man. In fact, she positively and actively *dis*liked Jake Emmerson!

Taking a deep breath, Oriel strove to put all disturbing thoughts about Jake firmly out of her mind as she gazed up at the castle looming high above her. The heavy grey stone edifice seemed somehow menacing as she moved further away from the car, making her way through the mass of heavy boulders to gain a closer look at the castle.

'It's really something, isn't it?' a voice said from behind her. Startled, Oriel turned to see Jake leaning casually against a rock as he, too, gazed up at the grim fortress. 'I guess there must be a fantastic view from up there. Although I still can't work out how those crusaders——'

They both jumped, looking at each other in surprise as they heard a loud, sharp *bang* coming from the direction of the limousine.

Oriel frowned. 'That sounds like a car's backfire, but——' She broke off as they both heard a high-pitched cry.

'Hell!' Jake exclaimed. 'That must have been a gunshot!'

A second later he had spun around on his heels and was running back towards the limousine. Dazed by the speed of events, Oriel followed his fast-disappearing figure, stumbling over the stony ground as she tried to weave her way through the maze of rocks. Suddenly finding herself at the edge of the clearing, she came to a sharp, juddering halt, her progress barred by Jake's outstretched arm as he stood grimly regarding the scene in front of him.

It was some moments before Oriel's dazed mind could fully comprehend the scene before her. There, leaning trembling against the side of the limousine, his face white with terror, was Halim Khaddour. Her eyes widened as she saw the reason for such alarm and fear. Standing beside the Minister, Laila Saliman was holding a revolver, whose barrel was pressed firmly up against Halim's head.

'For goodness' sake, Laila—what the hell's going on?' Jake demanded angrily. 'What do you think you're doing with that gun?'

'Don't move!' Laila called out as Jake took a threatening step forward.

'Don't be so damned stupid!' he retorted. 'What can you hope to gain by this nonsense?'

Laila gave a shrill, high-pitched laugh. 'My friends will soon be here. And then you will see that this is no nonsense!'

Oriel felt sick, her knees knocking together like castanets, and it was only Jake's firm hand now gripping her arm which prevented her legs from sagging beneath her.

'We can't just stand here,' she protested breathlessly. 'Surely we can do something?'

'Like what?' Jake murmured, his mouth tightening grimly as he noted the wicked-looking rifle leaning up against the car, only a few inches away from the chauffeur, who was calmly removing the suitcases from the boot of the car.

There were only twenty yards between himself and the car in the centre of the clearing, but it might have been twenty miles. There was nothing he could do to help the Minister—not while Laila had the gun pressed so closely to Halim Khaddour's head. Besides which, there was the matter of the chauffeur and his gun. If it had just been a case of Laila, Jake wouldn't have hesitated in trying to rush her—there was no way she could keep the gun trained on the both of them. However, while the chauffeur seemed oblivious to what was going on as he continued to calmly remove the suitcases from the car, with the rifle lying so close to him, Jake knew that he would be endangering Oriel's life as well as his own if he attempted to rescue Halim.

While Jake had been evaluating the situation, Oriel's fear and bewilderment had turned to rage.

'Jake's quite right,' she said angrily, disregarding Laila's shout of warning as she took some steps forward. 'What can you possibly hope to gain by pointing that beastly gun at poor Halim? And what's all this about your "friends" joining you in a few minutes?' she demanded, scowling at the other girl. 'Are you part of some sort of hijack gang—or what?'

'I have no time to discuss these important matters with you,' Laila retorted. 'If you know what's good for you, you will go back and stand beside Mr Emmerson.'

Oriel took only a small step backwards. 'Well . . . if you're expecting the rest of your gang to join you—it doesn't look as if you're going to have much luck. Not unless they've got a helicopter!' she taunted, waving her hand around at the mountainous terrain. 'Jake's quite right when he says that this is all a complete nonsense.'

Laila swore under her breath. '"Jake says","she mimicked Oriel's English accent. 'Mr Emmerson is even more stupid than you are! What can an American dog know, or understand, of our plans for the Glorious Revolution? What can either of you do against our superior moral force?' Laila's speech was becoming almost slurred in her fanatical excitement.

'When the other members of my organisation arrive, they will have no trouble with such weak, spineless individuals. And when Halim Khaddour is taken to Beyrouth—*then* the whole world will see the Minister for what he is . . . a lackey of the wicked imperialist forces who has betrayed the true faith!'

That girl's completely out of her tiny, rotten mind—as nutty as a fruitcake! Oriel was telling herself when Jake spoke from behind her.

'When you say "Beyrouth"—do I take it you mean Beirut . . .?'

'Yes, of course,' Laila snapped impatiently.

'Aagh!' the Minister groaned. 'What will become of my children—and my wives?'

'Beirut . . .?' Oriel spun around, gazing at Jake with consternation. 'I . . . I hadn't realised,' she muttered. 'I mean, I suppose the border isn't too far away, is it? Only sixty miles or so. Oh, hell! She can't really be meaning to . . .' Oriel turned back to Laila. 'You're going to kidnap him, aren't you' And when Laila merely laughed in assent, Oriel proceeded to lose her temper.

'You can't do this—you foul girl! I'm not going to let you get away with it!'

Laila gave another of her high-pitched, menacing laughs. 'Tell her, Mr Emmerson,' she hissed venomously. 'Explain to this stupid English woman that there is nothing she can do.'

Jake gave a heavy sigh. 'Laila is quite right, Oriel,' he said quietly. 'If you turn your head slowly to the left, you can see why.'

Disregarding his instructions, she spun on her heels, her action alerting the chauffeur, who immediately bent forward to pick up the rifle beside him, turning it menacingly on her nervous figure.

If she hadn't been feeling so frightened, Oriel would have screamed with frustration. Was there really *nothing* they could do to help the Minister? Surely there must be some way in which——? Her frantic thoughts were interrupted as her ears caught the distant sound of an approaching motor.

'Ah!' Her rock-steady hand still keeping the gun pressed against Halim's head, Laila glanced down at the watch on her other wrist. 'You see—it is as I said. My friends are arriving, right on time.'

As the sound of approaching engine became louder Jake muttered to Oriel, 'Get back over here.'

'What?' Oriel looked about her in confusion.

'Oh, for heaven's sake!' And a second later, as she saw a large grey truck beginning to turn into the clearing from the road, she found herself quickly grabbed by Jake, who swiftly dragged her back towards the shelter of the rocks.

'What are you doing?' she cried breathlessly, as he tore rapidly through the maze of rocks, towing her willy-nilly in his wake. 'Ouch—that hurt!' she gasped as she banged into one of the large boulders.

'Stop moaning!' he grated, not ceasing his rapid progress as they wound their way through the mountainous debris. 'If you think you are hurt now—wait until those guys back there get hold of you!'

'But where are we going?' she demanded

breathlessly, tears coming to her eyes as she
stubbed her toe hard against a large stone.

Jake ran around the side of two large rocks
bonded together in a V shape, and came to an
abrupt halt. 'This'll do,' he said, stepping
quickly inside the narrow, cavelike gap between
the two rocks and swiftly pulling her in beside
him.

Oriel gazed up at him, one part of her
frightened mind noting that he barely seemed
to be out of breath while she, herself, was
panting as if she had just run a mile. 'What are
we doing—running away like this? Surely there
was something we could have done to help
Halim?'

Jake sighed. 'At the risk of repeating
myself—like what?' he asked quietly. 'You don't
really think that they were going to just leave us
standing beside the road, do you? That nasty bit
of goods, Laila, might have had her gun on the
Minister, but once the rest of her gang turned
up you can bet your sweet life that we would all
have been carted off to Beirut.'

'*What*?' she shrieked.

'For heaven's sake keep your voice down!' he
hissed angrily.

'But why?' she whispered, her legs beginning
to shake again. 'What's the point? I mean——'

'There's no point,' he retorted roughly.
'There's no rhyme or reason behind the crazy
kidnappings that go on in Beirut. But that
doesn't stop them happening, does it?'

'No, but——'

'Look, you've got to face the facts. I might have been able to deal with Laila on my own. And, maybe, if we'd managed to keep her talking long enough, I could have found a way to outwit the chauffeur as well. But once that truck arrived I knew there was nothing I could do.'

'But we can't just stand here and do *nothing*.'

'For heaven's sake, Oriel—I'm not Superman!' he ground out with exasperation. 'I don't like having to run away and leave Halim to his fate, any more than you do. However, he may get lucky. As you know, the Syrians control half of the Lebanon, so they probably won't have any difficulty in ransoming the Minister. In fact, the chances are that they'll regard it as merely an embarrassing diplomatic incident. But the situation is very different as far as you and I are concerned. Don't forget that America has exactly the same attitude towards terrorists as you have, in Britain—no deals, and no ransom payments. So, if I can't save Halim, then I've no intention of standing around and waiting to be hauled off to some dark hell-hole in Beirut—where I'd be left to moulder until Kingdom Come!'

'Oh, it's like that, is it?' she hissed scathingly. 'This is all about the self-preservation of Jake Winthrop Emmerson III, is it?'

He stood looking down at her for a long moment. 'OK, sweetheart,' he ground out through clenched teeth. 'If you don't mind being locked up for years on end, and are quite willing to act as a sacrificial lamb, then why don't *you* go back and join your friend Halim, right now?'

Oriel glowered up at him. He really was a ruthless bastard! Of course she didn't want to be kidnapped and dragged off to some ghastly dark hole in Beirut. But neither did she want to feel that she was being a coward in abandoning the Minister. It was a no-win situation, and somehow—totally illogical though it might be—she couldn't help feeling that this was all Jake's fault.

'Well?' he demanded angrily.

'Oh, all right,' she relented. 'But I still feel——'
She could say no more as he placed a hand over her mouth and quickly drew her struggling figure towards him.

Swiftly lowering his dark head, he whispered urgently in her ear, 'For goodness' sake—be quiet! They're looking for us—so, whatever you do, don't make a sound.'

Standing as still as a statue, petrified with fear, it was some moments before she heard the sounds which his ears had already picked up. There was a crash of metal against stone, and the sound of a male voice talking in Arabic.

'We know you are there, Mr Emmerson,' Laila called out. 'However, we have no more time to waste, and without transport I do not think that either you—or the stupid English miss—will get very far!' she added with a spine-chilling laugh, which echoed eerily in the still, desert air.

Jake kept his hand firmly clamped over Oriel's mouth, his other arm pinning her shaking figure to his hard form, until a few minutes later when they heard the sound of a heavy vehicle being driven away.

'OK,' he said at last. 'I think they've gone.'

Having made their way slowly and carefully back through the maze of rocks and boulders, Oriel and Jake stood at the edge of the clearing, surprised to see that the scene before their eyes was little changed. The Minister's large black limousine remained standing peacefully in the centre of the clearing, only the pile of discarded suitcases at the rear of the vehicle providing evidence of the recent hijack.

'What idiots they are!' exclaimed Oriel. 'They've left us the car. Even if they've taken the keys, I bet we can still get it going, somehow,' she added excitedly. 'It won't take us long before we can get hold of some help for Halim.'

'This all looks too good to be true,' Jake said slowly, frowning as he stared at the car.

'Oh, for goodness' sake!' She gave a scornful laugh. 'You can look a gift horse in the mouth if you want to—but I'm certainly not going to.'

Oriel began walking towards the car, not heeding Jake's warning cry nor the sound of his pounding feet as he raced swiftly towards her. At the very moment that Jake reached Oriel, spinning her around and throwing her down on to the ground, there was a sudden, colossal

explosion in which she hardly had time to think
. . . to breathe . . . to feel anything—before the
whole world disintegrated around her.

CHAPTER FOUR

ORIEL was feeling warm and happy in the darkness. If only that person would stop making such a noise.

'Wake up, Oriel. At once!' the voice continued to demand sternly, before swearing roughly under its—his?—breath. 'Come on, you beautiful, impossible and quite infuriating girl, *wake up*!'

Through the dense, impenetrable mists swirling through her brain, she slowly began to recognise the deep, dark tones of the commanding voice in her ear.

'Go away,' she said, but the words which had been quite clearly defined in her head now sounded thick and slurred as she voiced them. She tried again. 'Go away, you horrid man.'

His only reply was a deep rumble of laughter. How dared he laugh at her? Fury and indignation gave her the impetus to open her eyes, although it was a second or two before the long, thin streaks of light widened sufficiently to dissolve away the grey mist and she could see the broad-shouldered figure bending over her.

'Hello—at last!' he said with a grin.

'I prefer the word "goodbye",' she muttered, before determinedly closing her eyes again.

Jake gently shook her shoulder, refusing to allow her to slip back into the comforting darkness. 'I'm sorry, sweetheart, but I'm afraid it's wakey-wakey time.'

'Kindly stop calling me "sweetheart",' she told him crossly, sighing heavily as she gave up the unequal struggle and reluctantly opened her eyes.

Jake gave a low, sardonic laugh as he bent forward to adjust the pillow beneath her head. 'OK, *Doctor*—I'll try to remember that important fact!'

Oriel was finding it practically impossible to think clearly. It was as if she was suffering from the after-effects of some deep anaesthetic, her brain a jumbled mass of incoherent thought-waves as she gazed muzzily up at the face only inches away from her own. She knew—only too well!—that he was a thoroughly horrid, untrustworthy individual. But, all the same . . . she thought groggily, he . . . well, he really was a quite sensationally attractive man.

'How about trying to sit up?'

'Sit up . . .?' she echoed, striving to pull her stunned senses together, and gradually becoming aware of the fact that she was lying on the ground. 'I don't understand—ouch!' She winced as she tried to move her head.

'Relax—you're OK. You've obviously had a bump on your head, and you've got a slight graze on your cheek and another on your leg, but you don't seem to have any other serious injuries,' he said reassuringly as he dabbed her face with a large white handkerchief.

'Where are we? What's happened?' she asked, a rising note of hysteria in her voice as she noticed for the first time that he had a small cut over one eye, and that his crisp white shirt was now ragged and streaked with dirt and . . . 'That—that's blood!' she cried, lifting a trembling hand to touch the bright red stain.

'There's nothing for you to worry about,' he said firmly. 'My back feels a bit sore, but I'll ask you to look at that later. Right now, I want you to try and sit up. You may feel a bit dizzy at first, but we're going to take it slow and easy, so there's no need to panic.'

'I have no intention of panicking!' she snapped.

He gave a bark of dry laughter. 'OK, iron lady, here we go.'

Oriel didn't panic. However, feeling slightly faint and giddy, she was grateful to have the support of his firm arms for some moments before the fog began to clear in her brain and she had a chance to look about her.

Apart from the high, towering walls of the crusader castle looming threateningly over them, as far as she could see they might as well be on the moon. The rough, sandy ground on which she was sitting was covered with small rocks. There was a distinct smell of burning in the air, and odd pieces of metal, twisted into strange grotesque shapes, lay scattered about the rocky surface.

'What on earth are we doing here?' she said in bewilderment as he reached behind her, and she realised that the 'pillow' which had been placed beneath her head was the dusty, torn jacket of what had once been his immaculately tailored suit. 'That was—er—that was kind of you,' she muttered.

Jake's mouth twitched at the note of surprise in her voice. 'I do have my moments, you know,' he said with a grin. 'How do you feel now?'

'All right—I think,' she murmured, raising a shaky hand to gingerly touch the large, painful lump on her head.

'Well enough to stand on your own two feet?'

'Hmm, yes, I think so,' she said as he helped her to rise. 'The last thing I can remember . . .' Her voice faltered as she looked about her with consternation. 'Where . . . where's the car?'

The small lay-by was completely deserted. The Minister's large black limousine seemed to have vanished into thin air. Where it had once stood in the centre of the clearing there was now a large depression in the ground, covered in charred, anonymous-looking lumps of material from which wisps of grey smoke rose slowly upwards in the still air.

'That can't possibly . . .?' she muttered, closing her eyes for a moment and shaking her head in disbelief. 'I know it sounds mad,' she added, turning to give Jake a quick, nervous smile, 'but, for one awful moment, I really thought——'

'You're quite right,' he said flatly. 'That, believe it or not, is what's left of the Minister's limousine.'

Oriel gasped, her blue eyes widening as she stared at the debris surrounding the blackened hole in the middle of the small clearing, and then turned back to gaze at the grim expression on Jake's face.

'I simply don't understand.' She frowned in puzzlement. 'I can remember that the car was sitting there. I think . . . yes, I can remember walking towards it, and then——'

'And then the bomb went off!'

'*A bomb*?' Oriel stared at him in horror. Feeling suddenly faint and dizzy, she took a stumbling step forwards, and would have fallen if he hadn't put out an arm to catch her. 'But why?' she whispered as he helped her to sit down on a nearby flat rock.

'I reckon it was a little goodbye present, from Laila,' Jake grated harshly as he contemplated what was left of the heavy vehicle. 'Yes, that girl sure is a *real* little darling,' he added grimly. 'It only came to me, when it was almost too late, that the terrorists—or whoever they are—would hardly be likely to leave us a method of escape. I only just managed to get to you in time. A few paces nearer to the vehicle, and I reckon that both you and I would have had it.'

'Oh, lumme! And I was just about to get into the car, wasn't I?' She paused. 'You . . . you've just saved my life, haven't you?'

He shrugged. 'I wouldn't get too excited about that,' he said flatly. 'We may have overcome one particular hazard, but things aren't looking too good, I'm afraid. This is hardly the Ritz.' He gestured around at the barren landscape. 'Goodness knows where we are, or how we get out of here and back to civilisation.'

Oriel gazed blindly up at him. She couldn't really think about the future—not just at the moment. She was still trying to come to terms with the fact that she had been so close to extinction, and, as the realisation of her incredibly lucky escape permeated into the far corners of her mind, she began to tremble and shake almost uncontrollably.

Jake quickly forced her head down between her knees, commanding her to take a deep breath. 'You're supposed to be a tough lady, so I don't expect you to start fainting on me, Oriel. Besides, my back is hurting like hell, and I want you to take a look at it.'

She took a deep breath. 'I . . . I'm all right,' she muttered, making a determined effort to control her trembling limbs. 'What's wrong with your back?'

'I don't know. That's why I want you to check it out,' he said, undoing the buttons of his shirt and wincing as he eased his shoulder out of the garment.

Oriel rose shakily to her feet. 'You'd better sit down on this rock, and I'll see what I can do.'

'I don't want anything fancy—and, in any

case, you're hardly equipped for a major operation,' he said with a wry laugh as he sat down on the rock with his back towards her. 'Just do the best you can, huh?'

She stared down at the thin red line cutting across the broad expanse of tanned skin from the edge of one shoulder down to the midpoint of his backbone. What on earth was she supposed to do? Oriel bit her lip with indecision, peering down at what appeared to be only a slight cut.

'I honestly don't know what to suggest,' she said helplessly, fervently wishing that she'd had some basic training in first aid.

'What do you mean?' Jake's voice was scathing as he turned his head. 'For heaven's sake—you're a doctor, aren't you? So, why don't you stop pussyfooting around, and get on and do some doctoring?'

Oriel stared down at his impatient expression, her brain a mass of confusion. 'I . . . I don't know what you're talking about. I'm not a doctor.'

'Of course you are!' he snapped curtly.

'No . . . no, I'm not. Well, yes, I suppose I am, in a way . . .' She sighed, brushing the hair from her brow with a trembling hand. 'You've made a mistake. I don't think you understand. I'm not a *medical* doctor. I'm a Doctor of Philosophy.'

'*What?*' He looked at her blankly, before snarling bitterly, 'Oh, great! That's *all* I need to make me feel a whole lot better. Here I am, stuck out in the middle of heaven knows where, with—guess who? A damned female Socrates!'

'No—no, you've got it all wrong,' she protested. 'My doctorate is nothing to do with that sort of philosophy. It's an honorary degree, awarded by Oxford University, for my thesis on—'

'I don't give a damn about Oxford—or Cambridge, for that matter,' he grated. 'All I want—if it isn't asking *too* much—is to know just what's wrong with my back,' he added with heavy sarcasm.

Oriel gritted her teeth, grimly forcing herself to count up to ten as she stared down at the cut scored across his tanned skin. It was obviously painful, she told herself, and therefore maybe she ought to try and be more sympathetic.

'You've got a slight wound which runs from here, to here.' She touched his skin briefly. 'As I've told you, I'm no doctor, but, if I had to hazard a guess, I'd say that you've been cut by a piece of flying metal. However, it isn't deep—not much more than a scratch—and I'm sure that, if you keep it covered, it should just heal naturally.'

'Thanks a bunch, sweetheart—for nothing!' he growled, picking up his shirt and rising to his feet.

Oriel glared up at him. She'd just about *had* this man—up to the neck! He might have saved her life, but the thought of having to be permanently grateful to such a bad-tempered, grouchy individual was just about more than she could stand.

'Look, I'm sorry your back is sore,' she said coldly. 'However, it's not the end of the world, is it? It's hardly *my* fault that I haven't been medically trained. In fact, if you'd bothered to check out my credentials, you'd have known——'

'Spare me the lecture!' he grated. 'The last thing I need at the moment is to have to listen to a bossy, opinionated girl who——'

'Don't be so rude!' she snapped, her cheeks flushed with anger. 'And anyway, at least *I'm* not a raving hypochondriac—making a song and dance about a small scratch,' she added with a contemptuous sniff.

Jake glowered down at her. '*What* did you say?' he demanded furiously.

Oriel backed nervously away from his threatening bare-chested figure. 'OK—OK,' she muttered. 'I didn't really mean it.' She sighed, and pushed a trembling hand over her hair.

He regarded her grimly for a moment, before putting on his shirt again and slowly doing up the buttons. 'Look here,' he said at last. 'It's nothing but a futile waste of time for the two of us to be quarrelling with each other. So, I suggest that we both just try and cool it, OK?'

Oriel stared back at him mutinously.

'You must see that we've got no option but to co-operate with one another,' he continued sternly. 'Heaven knows, I don't want to be unduly depressing, but the sooner you realise just what a predicament we're in, the better. And watching each other get dressed and undressed is going to be the very *least* of our problems,' he added with grim amusement, noting her embarrassment as he loosened the fastening of his waistband and began to push his shirt back inside his slacks.

Oriel gave a heavy sigh, quite convinced that she had never felt quite so desperately tired and exhausted. The sun, which seemed to be directly overhead, was beating down remorselessly on their two figures—so puny amid the stark landscape. She closed her eyes for a moment, grateful for a brief respite from the shimmering, glaring light which was reflected from the stony surface of the small lay-by. What had she ever done to deserve being stuck here, in the back of beyond, with a man who might have saved her life, but who had also made it very plain that he actively disliked her and found her a confounded nuisance?

Jake looked at the girl's tired, dejected figure, and was suddenly surprised to find himself feeling sorry for her. She had, after all, come through all this recent trauma with what he could only think of as remarkable fortitude. So maybe . . . maybe he had been a little hard on the iron lady . . .?

'I'm sorry if I've been a bit tough, but the sooner we both face the facts of the situation, the better,' he said quietly.

Oriel shrugged her tired shoulders. Jake was

absolutely the very *last* person she would ever have chosen to be stuck with on a desert island. And if this wasn't exactly the same situation, it came pretty close to it, if one substituted the encircling, grim mountain range for that of water. Still, it didn't look as if she had any choice in the matter. She and Jake were just going to have to get along together, somehow.

'You're right,' she said at last. 'I can't promise anything, but I'll try to keep my "cool" as you put it.'

'So will I!' he said, surprising Oriel by giving her a brief, friendly smile. 'I said I didn't want to be too depressing,' he added, his expression growing more serious, 'but I'm afraid that our situation can only be described as a very serious one. We have no food, no clothes, other than the ones we stand up in, and, most serious of all—we have no water.' He grimaced and brushed a hand roughly through his dark hair. 'I've been trying to remember exactly how much water the human body needs to survive. If I recall the statistics correctly, I think we're going to need about four pints per day.'

'As much as that?'

'Um-hmm.' He nodded. 'I'm afraid so. And that's another reason for conserving our energy and not quarrelling with one another.'

Oriel glared at him, but, after a brief mental struggle, she contented herself by merely saying, 'I don't see that there's any need for us to panic. It won't be long before someone comes down that road and rescues us, surely?'

'Like who?'

Oriel shrugged. 'How do I know? Just as long as it's got a wheel at each corner, I'll be quite happy to hitch a lift.' She gave him a scathing look. 'Of course, since you're *such* an important man, you may feel it's beneath you to travel in a truck, or whatever. But *I'm* quite prepared to hop into the first vehicle that comes along.'

Jake gritted his teeth. This uppity girl was driving him up the wall! Didn't she have any idea of just what a hazardous situation they were in? 'What vehicle?' he snorted with derision. 'This is clearly a very minor secondary road. So, the chances of any passing traffic—other than a herd of goats—is extremely unlikely. Right?'

Oriel bit her lip, reluctantly conceding that he was right. 'OK . . .' she muttered. 'But we can't just sit here. There must be *something* we can do to help ourselves.'

Jake gave her a sardonic smile. 'I'm glad to see that you're at last beginning to think in a straight line,' he said, rubbing salt in the wound. 'And you're quite right. It's pretty hot, just now, but I reckon that, up here in the mountains, it's likely to get very cold at night. So that means we're going to need shelter—and the obvious solution is to take refuge in that castle.'

She turned and raised her head, staring up at the grim fortress looming over them. 'You want us to climb up there?' she asked, trying to repress a shudder. 'How on earth do we get in?'

'Surely you must remember?' he said impatiently. 'The Minister told us that the castle had been recently restored. So there must be a way in, right?'

Oriel gasped. 'Oh—how awful!' she moaned. 'How could I . . .? How could I have forgotten about poor Halim? What on earth is going to happen to him?' she asked almost tearfully.

'I'm sure you've no need to worry,' Jake said in a firm, confident voice. He did, in fact, have severe doubts, but there was little point in sharing them with Oriel. The important thing at the moment was to try and keep the girl's courage up. 'The Syrian Government are bound to pay a hefty ransom for their Minister of the Interior. It would be a terrific loss of face if they didn't, and I imagine that they'll move as swiftly as possible. So, relax, hmm?'

'Well, if you're really sure . . .?'

'I'm absolutely sure,' Jake told her firmly. 'So, I reckon we'd better concentrate on our own predicament, don't you?'

Oriel was still worried about the Minister, but as Jake began issuing a stream of instructions she found her attention diverted to the immediate present. As much as she disliked being ordered around by him, she had to agree that his suggestion that they should search the area to see if they could find anything which might prove useful was a good idea. She was wandering disconsolately around the far side of the lay-by when she heard Jake's shout, which brought her running across to the edge of the small plateau.

'Now, this is what I call a miracle!' he grunted, climbing back up beside her, carrying the picnic hamper, which he had retrieved from the spot where it had fallen part of the way down the mountainside.

'The way our luck's going, I bet it's empty,' she said gloomily. But, to her surprise, and even though the contents had been somewhat tumbled about, the well-wrapped food did not seem to have been disturbed.

'O ye of little faith!' Jake grinned. 'Come on—let's see if we can find anything else.'

It took them some time, but, after a careful search of the lay-by, they did manage to find a few items which, like the picnic hamper, had obviously been blown out of the limousine when the bomb had exploded.

'Well, I guess something is better than nothing,' Jake said as they gazed down at the small pile of objects. 'Although I can't see much use for that!' he added with a laugh, tossing aside a brand new evening dress-shirt, still in its cellophane wrapper.

It was all right for him! Oriel thought glumly. At least they'd managed to find a further two completely unworn shirts of Jake's, as well as a slightly torn, dark red towelling dressing-gown, which he had also claimed as his. Unfortunately, despite searching high and low, there had been no trace of her suitcase or its contents. Their only other discovery had been a battered leather bag.

'I think these must be Halim's,' Jake said with a slight laugh as he held a short pair of trousers up against his tall figure. 'Still—they will at least give you a change of clothing.'

'Thanks a bunch!' she grumbled, grimacing at the sight of the voluminous waistband. 'How am I going to keep them up without a belt?'

'For goodness' sake—stop moaning!' Jake said impatiently as he picked up the spanner, crowbar and iron wrench, which he had discovered lying amid the ashes of the burnt-out vehicle.

'I feel entitled to have a good moan,' she retorted bitterly. 'I don't care about my clothes—but I'm really cheesed off about losing all my notes, and the films I took at Palmyra. My baggage insurance isn't going to cover those items, is it?'

He gave a short bark of caustic laughter. 'Your insurance, my dear girl, is the very least of our worries! So, let's not waste any more time,' he added briskly, handing her the Minister's bag while he gathered up the remaining items. 'The sooner we get a roof over our heads, the better.'

Oriel hesitated for a moment, gazing up at the grim old castle, which had survived in this desolate part of the world for the last eight hundred years. And then, with a sigh of resignation, she followed his tall,

broad-shouldered figure as he began making his
way through the mass of rocks lying at the base
of the mountain.

Half an hour later, after fording a narrow,
rushing stream and climbing up the last steep
part of the mountain on to a wide, grassy
plateau, Oriel came to a juddering halt.

'I can't!' she cried. 'I simply can't do it.'

'Sure you can,' Jake called out from the other
side of the bridge. 'It's a piece of cake!'

Oriel shuddered as she gazed nervously down
into the deep ravine which lay in front of the
castle. It must be almost a hundred feet to the
bottom, she thought, feeling faint and sick as
she looked down at the smooth, yellowish rock
surface of the deep, vertical walls. In the middle
of the ravine a tall, thin needle of rock, topped
with a few blocks of masonry, rose level with
the plateau and the entrance to the castle. The
narrow iron bridge which rested on the point of
the needle was the only route across the ravine
which stretched from between where she was
standing to Jake's tall figure on the other side.

It was a brilliant piece of engineering, of
course. The man-made ravine had been
deliberately cut, back in the twelfth century, by
the builders of the castle, who had clearly
realised that the weak point of the site was the
narrow neck of land which joined the rocky spur
on which the castle had been built to the
mountain plateau. And, of course, as soon as

she'd seen it, Oriel had immediately known where they were.

'It's Saladin's castle!'_ she'd exclaimed, mentally kicking herself for not having realised—despite all the research she had done before her trip to Syria—that this must be the famous inaccessible fortress of that great Muslim hero, Saladin.

'I don't know anything about this guy Saladin,' Jake had said, pausing for a breather from their stiff climb. 'But he sure chose a good site for this castle—I reckon it must have been invincible.'

'I should have realised . . .' Oriel had clicked her teeth with annoyance. 'It was built by the crusaders, and apparently Saladin only managed to capture it by planting spies in the castle. Once Saladin had got his hands on it, he never let it go, and it's not difficult to see why,' she had added, turning to look around at the mountainous terrain behind them.

'Yeah, well, I guess that's all very interesting—but I don't intend to stand here all day,' Jake had said firmly, before marching briskly across the fragile bridge towards the main entrance to the castle.

But now, as she stared down into the deep ravine, Oriel knew that she simply couldn't force herself to follow his example.

'Come on!' Jake shouted. 'Stop pussyfooting around and get yourself over here.'

'I can't!' she cried, closing her eyes for a moment

as she trembled with fear. 'I'm sorry . . . I simply can't face it.'

'Oh, for heaven's sake!' he ground out, marching swiftly back across the bridge towards her. And then, before she fully realised his intention, he calmly picked up her wriggling, protesting figure and strode determinedly back across the bridge.

Quite certain that they were going to plunge down into the perilous ravine below, Oriel could do nothing to prevent herself from shrieking with terror. She was still moaning when she felt herself being placed firmly on the ground, her legs buckling beneath her as she sank down on to a low rock, and promptly burst into a storm of tears.

Jake quickly bent down and gathered her into his arms.

'I . . . I'm so s-sorry,' Oriel sobbed helplessly. 'I d-don't know what's c-come over me——' She hiccuped.

'It's all right,' he murmured soothingly. 'You're quite safe now. Just relax and calm down, hmm?'

Oriel knew that she must try and pull herself together. But the effort required to do so seemed too much for her to cope with at the moment. Despite all the arguments and quarrels she'd had with this man, it was so comforting to be held within his firm embrace, to be able to rest her weary head against his broad shoulder, and savour the warmth and security of his hard, firm body.

'I feel such a f-fool,' she muttered.

'Relax, sweetheart,' he said softly, rocking her gently in his arms. 'I know that you're undoubtedly one very tough lady, but I didn't fancy walking across that ravine much myself, either. On top of which—you have just survived a bomb explosion, been knocked unconscious, *and* you've had several almighty rows with me.' He smiled down at the blonde head buried in his shoulder. 'That's more drama than most people come across in a lifetime, but you—you crazy, impossible girl—you seem to have managed it all within the space of a few hours!'

Oriel lifted her tear-stained face. 'Thank you for being so kind. I . . . I'm not really the crying sort of female, you know,' she assured him earnestly.

'Yes, I know,' he said, staring down into her blue eyes which were glistening with tears.

Thinking about the episode afterwards, Jake was *quite* sure that he had merely intended to give the poor girl a quick, friendly peck on the cheek. After all, she'd been through a very trying time, and was clearly in need of comfort and support, right? So, how was it that, once again—as had happened so often during this trip to Syria—matters had got so swiftly out of control?

For her part, Oriel, still feeling dazed and upset at the way she seemed to have gone so completely to pieces, had neither the will nor the energy to resist the cool, firm mouth descending to possess her quivering lips. Somewhere, at the back of her bemused mind, she was aware of a faint warning voice; but by the time her confused brain had decoded the message it was far, far too late.

Powerless to resist the sweet seduction of the lips moving over hers, she moaned softly, sliding her arms up about his neck and burying her fingers in his dark hair as she melted helplessly against him.

Her blind, instinctive reaction provoked an answering response as Jake's arms tightened convulsively about her slim figure, the deepening force of his kiss igniting a raging flame of sensual excitement which flowed like quicksilver through her veins.

His lips trailed down her arched neck, seeking the wildly beating pulse at the base of her throat, before he slowly raised his head and stared intently down into her brilliant sapphire-blue eyes.

'*Oriel!*'

The sound of his husky whisper broke through her bemused state. As she shivered with reaction to the storm of passion which his kiss had woken within her, a deep tide of crimson spread over her face as she realised that she was still clinging helplessly to his tall figure.

'I . . . I can't think what's come over me,' she muttered, her cheeks burning as she quickly snatched her hands away from around his neck.

Jake cleared his throat. 'It was just shock,' he

said quickly. 'Shock and—er—mental exhaustion. It's quite understandable, of course,' he added firmly. 'You've been through a great deal today. As for myself . . .' he raised his head, gazing up at the clear blue sky as if searching for inspiration ' . . . I was merely—er—concerned and worried about your state of mind.'

Oh, yes? Oriel stared fixedly down at his white shirt, which had not only been torn and stained by the explosion, but which was now looking thoroughly ragged after their climb up to the castle. How on earth was she going to extricate herself from this *very* embarrassing situation? Unfortunately, while one or two forceful, pointed remarks about his behaviour immediately came to mind, she was hardly in a position to argue about his version of events. After all . . . Her cheeks flushed as she realised that she had been kissing *him* every bit as enthusiastically as he had been kissing her! Besides which, if things had got a bit out of control—and they most certainly had!—well, it was far too late to do anything about it now.

'Look here,' Jake said firmly, clearly determined to change the subject. 'We've both had a hard day—to put it mildly—and not only are you obviously feeling tired and exhausted but, like me, I guess you're also probably in need of a good meal.'

At the mention of food her stomach gave a loud rumble and she realised just how hungry she was.

'Hmm ... yes, I'm starving,' she agreed, almost drooling at the thought of the food inside the large hamper which had been provided for the journey by her hotel in Aleppo.

'Right,' Jake said quickly. 'So, let's cart everything into the castle, and then we can start making ourselves comfortable.'

Following him through the arched entrance to the castle, Oriel was fascinated to note that they were passing beneath an old iron portcullis.

'Hurry up!' he called out impatiently as she paused to stare up at the iron grating held firmly in place by a rusty length of chain attached to the wall beside her.

'Oh, all right—I'm coming,' she muttered, following him into a large, central courtyard which seemed to cover the width of the castle. However, she barely noticed the shrubs and bushes, with their yellow, mauve and blue flowers, which seemed to be growing out of the stonework. All her attention—and that of Jake—was concentrated on the massive structure in front of them.

'How extraordinary! Why should anyone build a castle within a castle . . .?' Jake murmured, squinting up at the high turrets of the huge, square building.

'It's called a "keep",' Oriel explained. 'The main purpose of any castle was that of defence. So, even if enemy forces managed to get inside the main entrance, they still had to face yet another impregnable fortress.' She shrugged her shoulders. 'Quite honestly, trying to attack or lay siege to a well-guarded castle was a long, tiring business. As long as the inmates of the castle had plenty of food, and enough soldiers to man the defences, they could afford to just sit and wait for the other side to get fed up and go away. Of course, the enemy could try mining the foundations, but——'

'Thank you, Doctor.' Jake's dry, hard voice cut across her words. 'However, first things first—*if* you don't mind! Just at the moment, I am *far* more interested in food and shelter than in having to stand here in the hot sun and be forced to listen to a lecture.'

I really hate him—the sarcastic swine! Oriel thought viciously, her cheeks flaming with embarrassment at having been made to look such a fool. What on earth had she been doing, kissing him the way she had, just now? *She must have been out of her mind*! After all, he obviously didn't know very much about medieval castles, and all she'd been doing was answering a question he had raised. Well, it wouldn't be long before he discovered a few uncomfortable facts about life inside a castle. Just wait until he got thirsty, for instance. That would wipe the superior smile off his face! Because the chances of there being a reservoir in working order were very slim indeed. And even if it proved to be structurally sound, and containing water that was fit to drink, he still wouldn't have a clue where to look for it, would he?

Oriel knew she was being childish—but she didn't care! Flesh and blood could only take so much, and she had just about reached the end of her tether. As far as she was concerned, she couldn't wait for Jake Winthrop Emmerson III to realise that he wasn't *half* as clever as he obviously thought he was!

CHAPTER FIVE

ONE hour later, Oriel found herself prepared to take a slightly more charitable view of Jake Emmerson. It really was quite amazing how physical comfort could affect one's mental processes. There was no doubt, sitting beside a roaring hot fire, and filling her empty stomach with some food—at last!—that she was definitely feeling a whole lot better.

'Umm . . . this is *so* good!' She groaned happily as she sank her teeth into a portion of succulent cold chicken. 'And what a piece of luck, finding that pile of wood in a corner of the courtyard!' she added, gazing with pleasure at the roaring fire. 'Do you think it was left behind by the men restoring the castle?'

'I reckon it must have been,' Jake agreed. 'Although I could do with an axe, since many of the logs are too large to burn in this grate. However, we should be all right for a while, since there seem to be a lot of offcuts—maybe from various oak beams which needed repairing.'

Oriel leaned forward to help herself to a juicy tomato. 'Is there any coffee left in the thermos?' she asked hopefully.

'Well . . .' He hesitated for a moment. 'I think

we really ought to save what's left. I don't know about you,' he grinned, 'but I simply can't face the day without a cup of coffee first thing in the morning.'

He braced himself for the storm which he was certain would break about his head. The damned girl had done nothing but give him a very hard time ever since they had entered the castle. Whatever he had suggested had been absolutely wrong, as far as she was concerned! His insistence on a brief reconnoitre of what she referred to as the 'keep' had resulted in her becoming extremely grumpy and cantankerous. Although that was nothing to the storm of abuse and invective which had greeted his very sensible suggestion—once they had discovered the huge stone fireplace, on the second floor of the massive stone building—that they should light a fire before they investigated the contents of the picnic hamper.

Jake grinned wryly to himself as he recalled how Oriel had practically danced with rage when he had seized her purse and proceeded to tear up her cheque-book. But, as he'd pointed out, you needed paper and twigs to get a fire going—and what use was a book of blank cheques in this God-forsaken place? In fact, he was quite convinced that it was only because he was bigger and heavier than she was that he'd managed to persuade her to help him gather wood for the fire. Heaven knows, he didn't believe in violence. But it had crossed his mind

that if ever a girl deserved a good spanking—it
was Dr Oriel de Montfort!

However, to his astonishment he now saw that
she barely paused, between nibbling away at her
chicken leg, to nod at his suggestion, and agree
that maybe it was a good idea to conserve their
food and drink as long as possible. And if the
only way to get this pesky girl to behave in a
reasonable manner was to keep her tanked up
with food, then he could only hope and pray
that the contents of the picnic hamper didn't
run out too soon!

On the other hand, maybe he was being just
a little unfair. It had been a hell of a day for the
poor girl, and she had actually stood up to
everything with remarkable fortitude. Besides,
as she sat cross-legged on the stone floor, with
her cloud of long, blonde hair tumbling down
over her shoulders, Oriel looked simply
enchanting. And, however much he reminded
himself that she was undoubtedly trouble with
a capital 'T', he couldn't help remembering just
how good it had felt to hold her slim figure
within his arms, the yielding warmth of her full
breasts pressed against his chest, her slender
waist and the touch of her long, slim thighs
pressed so closely to . . .

Oriel, who had been rummaging in the wicker
picnic basket, looked up with surprise as Jake
leaped to his feet and began striding rapidly
about the large chamber. Oh, lord—he wasn't
going to get cross with her again, was he? She

wasn't normally frightened of anyone, or anything—other than that beastly bridge over the ravine outside, of course—but when he'd lost his temper and roared at her to 'stop belly-aching and go and fetch some wood for the fire—*or else*!', she had been so unnerved that she had immediately run to do his bidding.

She hated to think what her feminist friends back in Oxford would have said about her spineless reaction to such a male chauvinist demand, but they weren't stuck in this castle with him, were they? Besides, he might be a stuffy American banker, but he was also a remarkably handsome one. And she didn't buy that excuse he'd given her when he had kissed her so thoroughly outside the castle. If *that* was how he went around comforting women in shock, it wouldn't be long before he got himself arrested!

As she watched his tall, lithe figure as he paced about the room, her heart began pounding, heat flooding through her veins as she tried not to think about the erotic sensuality of his kiss, or the hard, firm arousal of the body which had been pressed so closely to her own.

'. . . that's going to be our major problem, and I can't think of a way of solving it.'

'Hmm . . .?'

'Oh, for heaven's sake! Haven't you listening to a word I've said?' Jake sighed, pushing a hand roughly through his thick dark hair as he stared down at her flushed cheeks. 'I was speaking about our main problem—how we're going to survive without water. Those cups of coffee were all well and good,' he gestured towards the thermos vacuum flask beside the hamper, 'but once we've drunk that we're in serious trouble.'

Oriel gazed at him for a moment, and then shrugged her shoulders. It was no time to play games, and they were both in this predicament together. With a sigh, she slowly rose to her feet. 'OK, I suppose we'd better go and see if we can find the reservoir.'

'What reservoir?'

'Where they kept the water, of course.'

'Who kept what water?' Jake demanded impatiently.

'The crusaders—of course. In its heyday, this castle would have contained at least one thousand men at arms, and all their horses,' Oriel said as she bent down and closed the lid of the picnic hamper. 'After all, you were the one who told me that human beings need four pints of water a day. So how do you think the knights—not to mention their horses, which must have drunk gallons of the stuff—survived up here?' She gave him a sardonic grin. 'They had to have a source of fresh water, and to be able to store it, didn't they?'

Jake swore under his breath. 'Of course!' He snapped his fingers in annoyance. 'Now, why didn't I think of that?'

A quick, sarcastic answer flickered through

her mind, but she just as quickly discarded it.
She didn't want to argue with him any more,
and he *had* been quite right about their need for
a fire. The sun might still be shining outside,
but it was at least twenty degrees colder inside
the thick stone walls of the castle.

'Oh, dear—oh, dear! It's very sad to have to
watch a clever, intelligent man's mind cracking
up,' she murmured, shaking her head in mock
sorrow. 'Still, never mind. If we ever get out of
here, I promise not to tell anyone how you went
completely to pieces!'

'Why, you little——' He strode quickly across
the room, bending down to seize her arm and
jerking her quickly to her feet.

'Relax! I was only joking.' She laughed
nervously.

'You weren't far off the beam,' he muttered,
staring down intently into her wide blue eyes. 'I
reckon that I may well be cracking up, and
there's a serious danger of my losing my mind,
too. Especially if we're alone here, together, for
much longer.'

Oriel suddenly felt breathless. Gazing up at
him, she noticed for the first time the glinting
silver lights in his piercing grey eyes, the hard,
sensual curve of his lips. Dazed and shaken by
the strange shivers of excitement racing through
her body, it was only the feel of his fingers
tightening on her arm which brought her back
to reality.

'I . . . I really was only joking,' she said quickly.

'And . . . I—um—I've been meaning to say that I'm sorry I was so grouchy about the fire. It is cold in here, and you were quite right about the need to keep warm.'

'Hey? Are you feeling all right?' He dropped his hand, one dark eyebrow raised as he gazed down at her with amusement. 'Dr de Montfort offering me an apology? Oh, boy—I guess you must be sick!'

'Not half as sick as I'll feel if we don't find any water,' she told him with a shaky grin. 'I hope you're prepared for the fact that the original cistern and reservoir could well be in ruins?'

'But, if restoration work has been carried on here, isn't it likely that they would have seen to the water supply?'

'Ah, that's a good point,' she murmured, relieved to find that she was slowly regaining her equilibrium, and that her legs weren't feeling quite so weak and feeble. 'Maybe you aren't losing your marbles, after all?' she teased.

'I wouldn't bet on it.' He gave a grim laugh before walking over to the spiral stone staircase which led down to the ground floor. 'Come on, let's go and see if we can find this reservoir of yours.'

Standing out in the courtyard between the keep and the entrance to the castle, Jake gazed up at the two main towers at each end of the outside wall. 'I'm trying to get my bearings,' he mused. 'Those towers and the wall are all we

could see when we were down on the road. I had
no idea this place was so huge,' he added,
turning around to survey the main bulk of the
castle behind him. 'I wonder what's on the other
side of the far walls?'

'A sheer mountain drop, I'd imagine,' Oriel
said before leaving his side to climb the outside
stone stairway which curved up around one of
the two outside towers. 'Hey! There's a terrific
view from up here,' she called down.

'I thought you were frightened of heights?'
Jake asked as he ran up the steps and joined
her on the ramparts.

'No, I'm not worried about heights. It's not
having something firm beneath my feet which
I can't stand,' she explained.

'That's perfectly understandable—I wasn't
mad about that bridge myself,' Jake said,
leaning over the edge to stare down at the deep
ravine which ran across the front of the castle
and effectively cut it off from the mountain
plateau.

'For goodness' sake, be careful!' she begged.
'Some of this stonework looks very loose and
dangerous.'

'OK, don't worry.' He stood up and turned
towards the wide rampart which led to the other
tower, frowning in puzzlement as he viewed the
large, square holes cut in the base of the stone
structure.

Oriel followed his eyes. 'Those holes were
built so that the crusaders could pour boiling

oil down on the heads of anyone trying to storm the castle,' she explained, grinning as he winced and made a face.

'They sure sound a bloodthirsty lot—how come you know so much about that period of history?'

She gave him a wry smile. 'I'd be in trouble if I didn't! After all, a lecturer in medieval history is expected to know *something* about the subject.'

'Is that why you're in Syria?'

'No, not entirely. I was officially invited to this country because my father, a well-known archaeologist, recently died here. However, since I've just finished writing a book about medieval warfare, I suppose I ought to be grateful for the opportunity to stay in this castle.'

'You speak for yourself!' He gave a sardonic bark of laughter. 'I can't wait to get out of this place! Incidentally,' he added, turning to lead the way down the outside staircase into the courtyard, 'I'm getting confused by all this business about crusaders, knights and Saracens. What were they all doing here, in Syria?'

'Well, you see . . .' she began, before pausing to smile and shake her head. 'Oh, no! I'm not falling into that trap. You'll only accuse me of lecturing you once again.'

He grinned. 'No—this is one time when I really *am* interested in hearing what you've got to say.'

'Wow—be still, my beating heart!' Oriel

laughed as she followed him across the courtyard, through the arched door of the keep, and into the main room, whose high-vaulted ceiling was supported by a large pillar.

'The word "crusade" comes from *crux*—a Latin word for cross,' she said, pointing to a large sign of the cross cut into the stone column. 'It was adopted by the European knights, who were Christian, in their attempts to seize the holy city of Jerusalem from the "Saracens"—a term applied to all those of the Muslim faith.'

'OK—that's clear enough. But why build a huge castle here—hundreds of miles from Jerusalem?'

'Because this long, rugged coastline was a major trade route between Europe and the Middle East,' Oriel explained. 'The leaders of the Christian forces poured men and arms into this area, building castles to guard the mountain passes, in order to first take and then hold the approach to what they called the Holy Land.'

'Rather them than me—this place gives me the creeps!' he murmured, walking across the dusty stone floor towards an arch in the far corner of the huge, dimly lit room. 'And it seems to go on forever,' he added as they progressed through one large room after another, before entering an enormous domed structure, which Oriel informed him had once been the main stable for the knights' horses.

'Look, you can see the indentations in the walls where there were once wooden mangers, and here——' She pointed to holes which had been drilled through the heavy pillars down the centre of the room. 'These are where they would have tethered the animals.'

'Fascinating,' Jake murmured, bending down to take a closer look. 'However, while I hate to remind you of the fact,' he added, straightening up and looking around him, 'we still haven't found any water.'

'The knights couldn't function without their horses, so it must be around here somewhere.' Oriel's voice echoed around the high-vaulted chamber, the same size and structure as a large cathedral.

Jake peered through the dim light. Where on earth had the girl got to now? But, just as he was opening his mouth to call out to her, he heard a triumphant shout. Following the sound, he made his way through a narrow passage before coming to a halt and staring with astonishment at the sight before him.

'Glory be!' he murmured.

'Well? Is this enough water for you?'

With Oriel's peal of laughter ringing in his ears, he gazed about him in amazement. It might be technically a reservoir, but it looked more like an ancient Turkish bathing place. The walls appeared to be covered in small blue mosaic tiles, with water running in a steady stream through a wide hole in the far wall, down into a small pool. From there, it trickled slowly over a low mosaic wall, and down into another, far larger pool.

'Isn't it lovely?' Oriel enthused. 'I can't wait to have a swim!'

'OK, let's not get too carried away,' he warned her. 'We don't yet know if this water is fit to drink.'

'Oh, pooh—who cares?' She laughed. 'I'm not going to sit around, dying of thirst, just on the off chance that this water isn't as pure as the driven snow. In fact,' she added with a grin, 'it probably is just that—snow from the high mountain peaks, which has melted and formed a river which the old crusaders must have tapped. We crossed over a stream to get up here to the castle, if you remember?'

Jake shrugged. She was probably right, he thought, and, in any case, she was also right about drinking the water. Without it, they wouldn't survive more than a day or two.

'It's damned cold in here,' he said with a shiver. 'It's been a long, hard day, and I reckon we're both pretty tired. So I suggest that we'd better get back and make sure that fire doesn't go out. We can explore the rest of this huge place tomorrow.'

By the time they had made their way back, Oriel was surprised to find it was growing dark outside.

'I'd forgotten how quickly the sun goes down in this part of the world,' she said, gazing out of the wide, arched window which looked down over the valley far below.

'Hmm . . . that reminds me,' Jake said, from the other side of the room, where he was investigating the contents of the battered suitcase. 'We'll have to conserve every drop of gas in my lighter—just in case this fire goes out and we need to light another one tomorrow.'

'We're lucky that you had a lighter on you, although I hadn't noticed you smoking any cigarettes,' she muttered, still staring out of the open window.

'I don't—only an occasional cigar in the evening. However, the point I'm trying to make is that we've no way of producing any form of artificial light.' He gave a rueful shrug as she turned around to face him. 'So, I guess we'll just have to go to bed at sunset, and get up at sunrise—as they used to do in the olden days.'

'Bed . . .?' She looked nervously around the room. 'I hadn't thought . . .'

'It's a case of the hard, stony ground, I'm afraid,' he told her. 'And you'd better put on as many of these clothes as you can. I'll try and build the fire up, but it may not last the night, and I'm pretty sure it's going to be damned cold in the early hours of the morning.'

Some time later, Oriel stood hovering uncertainly by the window. The only light in the room was that provided by the flames of the fire, and, peering through the darkness, she could see that Jake had been busy placing a thick row of folded clothes on the floor by the grate.

'Come on, Oriel, let's get settled down and go

to sleep.'

'Settled down . . .?' she squeaked, watching nervously as he moved to lie down on the pile of clothes. 'I really don't think——'

Jake sighed. 'Don't be so damned silly. I'm cold and tired, and, believe me, sex is the last thing on my mind! And, quite frankly,' he added as she made her way slowly and hesitantly across the floor towards him, 'I don't have enough strength to force my way through all those garments you're wearing!'

Oriel stood awkwardly in front of him, grimacing as she stared down at the pair of bright blue trousers, which she could only keep up by hanging on to the waistband, and which still came nowhere near her ankles. 'I don't know how Halim could bear to wear anything so revolting. I look just awful,' she moaned unhappily.

'No, you don't. In fact, I think you look cute in those trousers,' he murmured. 'Now, for heaven's sake, stop messing around, and let's get some rest.'

Oriel hesitated for a moment, and then gave a weary sigh. She, too, was cold and tired, and it was childish of her to imagine that Jake had anything else on his mind but a decent night's sleep. Besides, dressed up in this weird assortment of clothes, she felt about as attractive as a huge wad of cotton wool. Lowering herself down on to the makeshift mattress, which was far thinner and harder than she had imagined it would be, she gingerly edged her body away from Jake's.

'Oh, sweetheart, don't be such an idiot!' he sighed softly, putting out his arm to pull her stiff figure into his arms. 'Now, go to sleep,' he said, firmly settling her head against his broad shoulders. 'And just remember that hard-nosed American bankers—such as myself—are only interested in "figures" that add up into dollars and cents!'

She gave a small grunt of amusement as she relaxed against his strong, firm body. Very surprisingly, considering the antagonism which had sparked so frequently between them, she now felt totally relaxed and safe with the comfort of his arms about her, and within minutes she was fast asleep. But, for Jake, staring blindly through the darkness at the ceiling high above him, and trying to ignore the soft warmth of the body pressed so closely to his own, it was a long time before he, too, fell into a restless, disturbed slumber.

The pale light of dawn was lighting the sky when Oriel opened her eyes. It took her some moments to remember exactly where she was, and then she became sharply aware of both her sore, aching body and the heavy weight which was pinning her down on to the hard stone floor. She raised her head slightly and her eyes widened at the sight of the dark head lying between her breasts. *What on earth . . .?* Oh, of course. She slumped back on to the thin clothing, which was all that lay between her and the cold stone beneath, and turned her head to gaze at the smouldering ashes in the large fireplace. As full memory returned she tried to wriggle into a more comfortable position, raising a hand to try and push Jake's heavy body off her slim figure. Her action achieved nothing, other than a deep, muffled groan as he settled himself more comfortably on her body, and raised a hand to clasp her breast, his fingers tightening possessively about its soft, full curve as she gasped and tried to squirm away from his intimate touch.

Oh, lord—what was she supposed to do now? If she gathered up all her strength she could, possibly, manage to push him away, but the stone floor must have been far more uncomfortable for him—especially with that long scratch across his back. Even as she framed the thought in her mind, Oriel knew that she was feeling too tired and exhausted to make the effort. Besides, Jake obviously wasn't interested in her as a woman at the moment—what he clearly wanted was a soft, warm pillow! She wouldn't mind having one, either. In fact, what they both needed were some palliasses, she told herself sleepily, before slowly drifting off into a deep slumber.

When Oriel woke again, it was to find shafts of bright sunlight slanting in through the open window. Raising her arm, she squinted up at her wrist-watch. Ten o'clock. Good heavens! How on earth had she managed to sleep that long? she wondered, groaning out loud as she eased her aching body up into a sitting position. Brushing the tousled hair from her brow, she looked about the empty room.

There was no sign of Jake, and neither was there any evidence that she had spent the previous night sleeping with a man. Her cheeks flushed as she remembered the weight of his hard, firm body, and the way his hand had clasped her breast. Oh, come on! she told herself roughly. Even if she had never slept with a man before, it was patently ridiculous for her to be feeling so embarrassed. It wasn't *her* fault that she and Jake had ended up in this extraordinary castle, and if she hadn't had a great deal of sexual experience—well, that wasn't her fault, either.

Her Aunt Harriet, that general do-gooder, well-meaning philanthropist and raging feminist, had been extraordinarily repressive as far as Oriel's love-life had been concerned. 'There'll be no hanky-panky in this house!' her aunt had declared when she had caught her niece kissing a boy goodnight on the doorstep. And so, mainly because she was so fond of her aunt, and had felt a deep debt of gratitude to the woman who had brought her up, Oriel had managed to reach her present advanced age of twenty-five with only one serious romance to look back on. And, of course, there had been her work, which she had found so rewarding that she barely grudged the large amount of time spent poring over old documents inside dusty libraries.

So maybe that was why, when she had met Chris Fitzgerald, a research student from Dublin, she had fancied herself so deeply in love. But, although it had been high summer when they had first met—a summer spent going for long walks through the meadows surrounding Oxford, and lazily drifting in a punt down the Isis—by the time cold winter had arrived it had become apparent that both she and Chris, who was heavily involved in his studies on atomic physics, had little or nothing in common. Just like herself and Jake, she thought, and then wondered why she should be feeling so unaccountably depressed.

'Ah, you're awake, I see,' Jake said, coming into the large room, carrying an armful of logs.

'I was wondering where you had got to,' she murmured, watching as he bent down to put some of the smaller pieces of wood on the smouldering ashes.

'I've been for a swim in the reservoir,' he said, placing the rest of the wood beside the large grate before rising to his feet and walking across the room to fetch the thermos of coffee. 'It was great to feel clean again, but I must warn you that the water is *very* cold!' He turned his head to grin at her. 'After that icy swim, I was supremely grateful that my dressing-gown wasn't blown up with the rest of my clothes. Although I could certainly do with a razor,' he added, grimacing as he raised a hand to rub his chin.

Gazing up at his tall figure in the short, dark red towelling gown, Oriel suddenly felt quite sick with . . . well, she wasn't quite sure what. Maybe it was the sight of his long brown legs, or the display of so much of his tanned chest, with its liberal sprinkling of dark, curly hair, which was making her feel suddenly so weak and breathless. The fact that he was quite clearly stark naked beneath the towelling wrap wasn't helping to calm her rapid pulse, either. Although why she should suddenly be feeling so peculiar, she had absolutely no idea.

'I found this in a corner of one of the downstairs rooms,' he was saying as he held up a small, battered saucepan. 'I imagine that it must have been thrown away by one of the men working here on the restoration of the castle, and I thought it would be just the thing to boil up some coffee. It's OK,' he added quickly as she wrinkled her nose. 'I took it along to the reservoir and gave it a good clean.'

'If that's the only way I can get a hot cup of coffee, I don't care *what* state it's in!' She smiled. 'I hope we get rescued soon, because the thought of having to face tomorrow morning without any coffee is almost more than I can bear to contemplate!'

'That makes two of us,' he agreed.

'How long do you think it will be before we are rescued?' Oriel asked as he knelt down to place the saucepan in the fire.

Jake shrugged. 'It all depends on how soon my young aide, and the Minister's guards, manage to raise the alarm. I'm sure we won't be stuck here for too long,' he added reassuringly. 'Have you got anyone waiting for you in Damascus?'

'No. I've been touring Syria on my own.'

'How about your family, back in England?'

She shook her head. 'My father's dead, and my only relative is an aunt, who's in Africa at the moment.'

'Africa? That's a bit off the beaten track, isn't it? What's she doing there?'

Oriel hesitated for a moment, but, since he did seem to be genuinely interested, she began telling him about her eccentric father, and her equally eccentric aunt, Harriet Turnbull.

'I promise not to call you "crazy" ever again!' Jake laughed. 'It sounds as if you've got a long way to go before you catch up with your aunt. I don't want to be rude, but a house full of political refugees, *and* a number of battered wives plus children, sounds my idea of sheer hell!' He shook his head, his shoulders heaving with laughter. 'How on earth do you manage to do any work?'

'With difficulty!' She grinned. 'Still, I'm proud of the work Aunt Harriet does for Amnesty International, and of her efforts to help the battered wives she takes in—the violence that some of those women have faced is truly awful,' she assured him. 'If I want any peace and quiet, I can always escape to my rooms in college.'

'And is there a handsome boyfriend anxiously awaiting your return?' he asked casually as he removed the saucepan from the heat.

'No—no one special,' she muttered, watching as he poured the hot liquid into the plastic cups which had been removed from the picnic hamper. Quite inexplicably, she suddenly found herself wishing that she had a whole hoard of terrific-looking, vitally interesting and amusing boyfriends to dangle in front of Jake. But the men she had been dating over the past few months—two history dons and a philosophy tutor—while interesting, were, unfortunately, *not* the answer to a maiden's prayer.

'And what about you?' she asked as he leaned forward to place a cup in her hands. 'I know that you're a banker, and something big in the IMF, but that's about all.' She hesitated, trying to remember what Mary Lou had said about his ex-wife. 'I—er—I gather you've been married . . .?'

'Yes, I certainly have.' Jake sighed, staring down at his cup of coffee. 'And what a mistake that was.'

'Oh, dear. I shouldn't have said——'

'That's OK. I was a bit bitter about it at the time, but, if I'm honest, I'll admit that the breakdown of the marriage was mostly my fault.' He shrugged his shoulders. 'I was—and maybe still am—what is referred to as a workaholic. We were both very young. Barbara was only interested in having a great social life, and she definitely didn't want any children. So, when she ran off with an Argentinian polo player . . .' He turned his head to give her a wry smile. 'Well—I can't say that I made much of an effort to get her back.'

'I'm sorry.'

'There's no need to be, because it all happened a long time ago, and it taught me a good lesson. Nowadays, I try to remember that there's more to life than columns of figures, or studying a company's financial records. However, right now,' he grinned, 'I can't help feeling that a course in survival training would have been a far more useful lesson!'

He rose and walked slowly over to the open window, staring out at the mountainous terrain in silence for a moment, before turning back to face her.

'I wasn't entirely joking about survival training—because the situation doesn't look too good, I'm afraid,' he said heavily. 'The food in that hamper won't last us more than two more days, at the most. And, while I don't want to alarm you, I think we've both got to face the fact that the hijacking of the Minister was fairly meticulously planned. I very much fear that we haven't seen the last of that girl Laila, nor the rest of her gang.'

CHAPTER SIX

SITTING on a large stone in the courtyard, one hour later, Jake glanced down again at his watch. Where on earth had that girl got to? Time wasn't, of course, very important—after all, they had nowhere to go and no one to see. But, over the years, hard work and accurate timekeeping had become, as far as he was concerned, practically an article of faith, and he was finding it very difficult indeed to relax and do nothing.

Women! They were all the same, he told himself, glancing down at his watch again. Goodness knows, he'd tried to explain the very serious difficulties they were likely to face, but Oriel had appeared to be remarkably unconcerned about the problems in store for them. In fact, it had taken him some time to convince her that the diversion sign, which had caused the limousine to leave the main highway for the secondary road below the castle, hadn't been an accident of pure fate.

'Of course it was planned,' he'd told her firmly. 'Do you really believe that a truck, full of armed desperados, just happened to come along at *precisely* the right moment? There is no way it could be a coincidence—and the sooner you accept it, the better.'

'Oh, all right,' Oriel had conceded. 'But I still don't see why you think that awful girl Laila and the rest of her gang are likely to come back here.'

While Jake had agreed that there was a slight chance that they might not, he'd felt bound to point out that Laila was undoubtedly part of a much larger organisation. And that when her colleagues realised that they'd let a rich American banker slip through their fingers—and, with him, the possibility of a very large ransom—he was almost sure that the temptation to return and capture the said American banker would prove irresistible.

However, even the prospect of such a dangerous situation had failed to dent Oriel's optimism. 'We'll just have to face that problem when we get to it,' the irritating girl had retorted briskly, before holding up a slim metal tube. 'If we get desperate for food, we could always eat my lipstick. I quite forgot to tell you that when I first left the limousine I took my handbag with me.' She gave him a rueful grin. 'You know how it is—a woman and her handbag are *never* parted!'

'Handbag . . .? Do you mean your purse?'

'They say that America and Britain share the same language—but I have my doubts about that,' she muttered drily, emptying the contents of her handbag on to the floor beside her. 'I seem to have got everything in here but the kitchen sink. Although I'm not entirely sure whether any of it is going to be of much use.'

Wasn't there something about the contents of a woman's purse accurately reflecting her mind? If so, Jake was sure that Oriel would provide a field day for a psychiatrist! However, he'd merely agreed that the scissors, small sewing-kit, long piece of string and the safety pins might well prove to be helpful. Although he couldn't see any use in the other aids to modern life, such as her bunch of keys, packets of tissues and a wallet containing her credit cards.

'You never know what might come in handy,' she'd told him cheerfully, replacing the collection of miscellaneous objects in her large leather handbag before announcing that it was time she had a wash and got dressed.

Glancing down at his watch again, Jake sighed and shook his head. Oriel really was a mass of contradictions. Take all that grumbling and moaning yesterday, when he could have quite cheerfully wrung her neck. And yet today, when life was clearly beginning to get immeasurably harder, the astonishing girl was being quite remarkably cheerful. Especially if one took into account what must have been a most uncomfortable night . . .

A slight flush covered his tanned cheeks as he recalled how he had woken up to find himself sprawled across her soft body. Thank goodness she'd been fast asleep, and could have had no knowledge of their close, intimate position. He couldn't imagine his ex-wife, any of his old

girlfriends, or the highly suitable blue-blooded
Marcia Lowell—who had been dangled in front
of his nose by both her parents and his elderly
mother for the past year—surviving the sort of
mess in which he and Oriel now found
themselves. But, sitting cross-legged on the floor
this morning, wearing a rag-bag selection of
clothes from the Minister's suitcase, and without
the benefit of make-up or the use of a comb with
which to tame that cloud of tangled blonde
curls, Oriel had, nevertheless, still managed to
look extraordinarily beautiful.

For heaven's sake—pull yourself together,
Emmerson! he told himself roughly. That girl is
nothing but trouble! Quite apart from being
half-drowned in the pool at Damascus, it was a
miracle that you didn't break every bone in your
body when she pushed you into the pit at
Palmyra—remember? But all he could remember
was the yielding warmth of her soft body when
she had fallen into the pit beside him—the same
sweet, velvety warmth which had been snuggled
so close to him last night, and . . .

'I'm sorry to have been so long,' Oriel called
out breathlessly as she ran into the courtyard.

Jake turned around at the sound of her voice.
'Good lord!' he exclaimed, rising slowly to his
feet.

'Yes, well . . .' She grinned sheepishly at him.
'I haven't got anything else of my own to wear,
and I couldn't face having to put on yet another
pair of Halim's dreadful trousers—not without

doing something about them. And since I found those scissors in my handbag . . .' She glanced down at what had once been a pair of bright jade-coloured trousers, and which were now a *very* short pair of shorts. 'You don't think I look too rude, do you?'

'*Rude?*' he croaked huskily, and then cleared his throat. 'No, I think you look—er—just fine.'

'Well, that's all right, then.' She beamed up at him. 'Let's explore those bits of the castle we didn't see yesterday, OK?'

'Yeah, sure . . .' he murmured, trailing slowly after her as she led the way towards the old gatehouse at the entrance to the castle. If they weren't rescued very soon, he told himself gloomily, it looked as if he was definitely going to become a victim of high blood-pressure.

Not only did those long, long legs of Oriel's seem to start from somewhere beneath her shoulders, but it was patently obvious that she was wearing nothing beneath the thin shirt which she had knotted in front, at her waist. And as for that *very* brief pair of shorts she was wearing! He closed his eyes for a moment, taking a deep breath as he struggled to control the lust rampaging through his body at the delicious, tantalising sight of so much bare flesh.

'Hey! We didn't see this when we arrived yesterday,' Oriel called out from somewhere within the dark recesses of the castle entrance.

As he joined her, he noticed that they had

indeed missed seeing the obviously new oak door set in the side of a wall. Pinned to its surface was a small notice-board, covered in Arabic script and also . . .

'What's that word?' He peered down at the board.

'It's "*Musée*"—French for "museum",' Oriel explained. 'The French virtually ran Syria until well after the war. Even today the street signs in Damascus are in both Arabic and French. And, of course . . . Oops, sorry!' She giggled as she caught the glint in Jake's eye. 'It looks as though I'm teaching my grandmother to suck eggs!'

'If that quite extraordinary expression means that you're lecturing me again—you're quite right!' he told her grimly. 'In any case, whether the language on that notice is in French, English or Hindustani is totally immaterial. There's no way we can possibly find out what's inside there.' He pointed to the brand new Yale lock. 'A pity—but there it is.'

Oriel glowered at the door. It wasn't just a pity—it was absolutely maddening. Because, if the people renovating the castle had bothered to lock the door, there must be something inside worth stealing. Well, she wasn't going to let a little thing like a Yale lock stop her.

'Come along. There's no point in hanging around here any longer,' Jake was saying impatiently when she suddenly had a brilliant idea.

'Don't move—I'll be right back,' she called out

as she took to her heels and ran swiftly back across the courtyard. And, as good as her word, in a very short space of time she returned, waving a small leather wallet in her hand. 'Thank goodness I held on to my handbag,' she told him breathlessly as she extracted one of the plastic credit cards from the wallet. 'What luck! I've read about burglars and detectives opening locks with one of these, and now I'll be able to see if it really works. Have you ever done it?'

'Good lord—no!' He frowned with heavy disapproval. 'Quite apart from anything else, what you're intending to do is thoroughly illegal.'

'Oh—don't be so stuffy. And, anyway, I thought we were supposed to be trying to find some way of saving our skins. If that awful girl Laila is going to turn up here again—well, it certainly won't be *my* fault if I can't make her wish she hadn't been born!' Oriel added viciously.

'Oh, yes?' Jake gave a snort of derision. How dared she call him 'stuffy'? 'And just what are you hoping to find in there? A few Soviet Kalashnikov AK rifles? Or maybe a box of grenades?' he added with a patronising laugh.

'The trouble with you, Jake, is that your mind is still firmly rooted in the twentieth century,' Oriel muttered, trying to concentrate on opening the door. 'But since we're stuck here in this castle, with no modern aids of defence to hand, I reckon that the sooner we begin thinking like the twelfth century knights who had to defend this fortress—the better.'

Leaning back against the rough stone wall of the passage, and thoroughly enjoying the sight of Oriel's slim figure as she bent down and fiddled with the stubborn lock, Jake smiled and shook his head. She was, of course, completely crazy. Even if she managed to find a few rusty swords, what on earth did she think they were supposed to do with them? The last time he had played at being one of the Three Musketeers he must have been all of eight or nine years of age, for heaven's sake. As for her mad idea that she could somehow use one of her credit cards to open that lock . . .

'*Got it*!' Oriel shouted with triumph, pushing open the heavy door and then turning to give him a wide grin. 'Come on—confess! You never thought I'd be able to do it, did you?'

Jake's lips twisted into a wry grin. 'Having been exposed to the full flavour of your extraordinary personality, I must tell you that nothing you do surprises me any more,' he drawled smoothly. 'Absolutely *nothing*!'

'In other words, "no", you *didn't* think I could do it.' She laughed before disappearing inside the dark, cavernous room.

'OK, where's the tank and the armalite rifles?' Jake enquired as he joined her, raising a dark cynical eyebrow as he gazed about him.

Poor Oriel, this clearly wasn't what she had hoped to find, he thought, his gaze moving over the collection of rusty oil drums and some hessian sacks. Not that she seemed to be particularly disappointed. Squatting down on her heels, Oriel was humming happily under her breath as she sorted through a pile of debris in the far corner of the room.

'Hey—how about this?' she called out, picking up an axe which clearly had seen better days. 'Now you can cut up some of those larger pieces of wood. And I'm sure we can think of something to do with that,' she added, pointing to an old rubber tyre propped up against the far wall.

'Yeah, well—I guess the axe is OK, but as for the rest . . .?' Jake shrugged.

'Oh, for heaven's sake—don't be so pessimistic. There's a lot we can do to help ourselves. In fact, if we're stuck here for some time, we could even reconstruct a crossbow from some of these bits and pieces,' she told him, brandishing a flat, rusty piece of iron and some equally rusty coiled springs. 'These must have been found when they were restoring this castle. Now, if we could just make a wooden stock, and . . .' She paused, gazing up at him hopefully. 'Are you any good at carpentry?'

'No, I'm not,' he said firmly. 'And I'm no Robin Hood, either.'

Oriel shook her head impatiently. 'Robin Hood—if he ever existed—would have used a longbow, like present-day archery. I'm talking about a crossbow, which is *quite* a different weapon. It fired these iron bolts,' she explained, picking up a bundle of pointed metal rods, about nine inches long. 'Crossbows were regarded as a fearsome weapon in the Middle Ages. Accurate up to a hundred yards, and able to pierce heavy steel—they were absolutely lethal!' she added with a ghoulish smile.

'That's all very interesting, but——'

'How about us making a mangonel? Or maybe a trebuchet? Now, that really was a *terrific* weapon!' she enthused. 'All we need is a long, heavy piece of wood, balanced like a see-saw, and then we lob some heavy rocks over the castle walls on to Laila and her——'

'No! Crossbows and treb-whatsits are definitely *out*,' he retorted firmly. 'I've never known such a bloodthirsty girl. I can see that, any minute now, you'll be trying to come up with the medieval version of the atom bomb.'

'That was gunpowder. And, unfortunately,' she sighed regretfully, 'I'm afraid I don't know how to make it.'

Jake laughed. 'Well, that's a relief!' he said as she stood up, carrying her various bits of metal over to a small desk beneath the long, thin slit window.

'I know you think I'm being silly,' she said, perching herself on the edge of the table, and brushing the dust and flakes of rust from her hands, 'but if Laila and her gang do intend coming back to kidnap us, then we've got to find some method of defending ourselves. As I see it . . .'

But Jake wasn't listening as he stared at her sitting on the edge of the table, idly swinging her long legs back and forth. What was it about this girl? Like all true blondes, she had very white skin. And although all the women of his acquaintance seemed to spend hours trying to obtain a deep, mahogany tan, he was finding the sight of her long, pale limbs quite extraordinarily erotic.

' . . . so at least we can sleep more comfortably at night.'

'Hmm?' He looked at her blankly.

'Honestly! I don't think you've been listening to a thing I've said,' she muttered impatiently. 'I was saying that now we can make some palliasses, we can——'

'Hold it there,' commanded Jake. 'What do you mean, "pally-asses"?'

'I'm not suggesting that we should try and find some friendly donkeys!' Oriel giggled. 'I meant that now we can make ourselves some old-fashioned straw mattresses, or—more accurately, in our case—sacks stuffed with hay.' She pointed to the pile of old hessian sacks in the corner. 'I don't know about you, but, after spending last night on that cold stone floor, I'm still aching all over.'

'I get the idea—and it's not a bad one,' Jake acknowledged. 'Unfortunately, there's a major problem—we don't have any hay.'

'Ah, I've already got the answer to that.'

'I just bet you have!' Jake muttered with grim resignation. 'OK, I know I'm going to regret asking this question—but where do we find the hay?'

'Well, I thought that if we picked handfuls of that long grass on the plateau outside the castle, and left it to dry in the hot sun for a bit, then we could stuff these sacks,' she said. 'I know it's not *really* "hay", but at least we'd be more comfortable than we were last night. Or don't you think it would work?' she added, suddenly feeling strangely nervous as she noted the harsh, forbidding expression on his face as he stared down at the pile of sacks.

Jake, who had been trying *not* to think about how he had spent last night, cushioned by her warm, soft body, made a determined effort to pull himself together. 'Yes,' he agreed, walking over and picking up some of the rough sacks. 'I reckon you're right.' He turned and began moving towards the door. 'Come on—you maddening, and quite impossible girl—let's go and make hay while the sun shines!'

Oriel laughed as she followed his tall figure out of the room. He really did have quite a sense of humour beneath that handsome, stuffy exterior. Although, now she came to think about it, he hadn't been at all stuffy since they'd arrived at the castle, had he?

Oriel lay back in the long grass, closing her eyes against the hot sun which blazed overhead in the azure-blue sky. Her back ached, and her hands were still feeling sore from the hard labour of bending down and having to pull up enough grass to fill the four sacks. Although Jake had managed to gather twice as much as she had, she reminded herself. And she hadn't really been able to grumble about the hard work, because it had been her own rotten idea in the first place!

'How about a nice, cold drink of water?'

She opened her eyes and struggled to sit up, blinking as she gazed up at the tall figure looming over her—a dark outline etched by the scorching rays of the sunlight which was almost blinding in its intensity.

'I thought I'd go back and fetch some water in the thermos,' he explained, squatting down beside her and unscrewing the cap from the vacuum flask. 'It also seemed a good idea to place the picnic hamper in the reservoir,' he added. 'It's far and away the coldest place in the castle, and it may help to preserve the food—*ouch*!' He raised a hand and rubbed his eye.

'What's wrong? Are you hurt?' she asked with concern.

'I'm fine. I've just got something in my eye,' he muttered, vigorously rubbing his closed eyelid.

Oriel knelt up. 'Here, let me have a look,' she said, putting her hands on his shoulders as she peered closely at his face.

'No, I'm all right,' he said hastily.

'Oh, don't be so silly. I expect it's just a small fly,' she said firmly, leaning forward and ignoring his muttered protest as she raised a hand to remove the small black object which she could see in the far corner of his eye.

At the touch of her cool fingers on his cheek, Jake jerked his head backwards, and, since he had been squatting down and balancing on the balls of his feet, the result of his quick action was that he lost his balance. Feeling himself toppling over backwards, he quickly and instinctively grabbed hold of Oriel, and a moment later he was lying on his back with her still clasped in his arms.

'What the hell . . .?'

'Oh, lumme!' she gasped, staring wide-eyed down at Jake's tanned features, only a few inches away from her own. 'I don't know what happened . . .' she muttered, trembling as she felt his hands beginning to tighten about her waist. 'I think that—um—the fly, or whatever it was, has—er—gone now,' she added, feeling extraordinarily nervous as he remained silent, continuing to regard her with a grave and increasingly stern expression on his face.

And then, in the brief space between one quick heartbeat and another, he swiftly raised his hands and buried them in her cloud of thick golden hair, pulling her head fiercely down towards him. The mouth possessing hers was firm and warm, and as her lips parted beneath the insistent pressure of his tongue he gave a deep groan and rolled her quickly over on to her back.

There seemed to be a strong roaring noise in her ears, the blood pounding through her veins as she became consumed by a driving force slowly slipping beyond her control. As his kiss deepened she was oblivious to everything other than the loud thud of his heart hammering in unison with her own, and the hard strength of the long, lean body pressing her so fiercely down on to the ground. She was hardly aware of the helpless moan of protest which broke from her throat as his lips left hers, trailing his mouth down the long arch of her neck to the soft, scented hollows at her throat.

'*Sweetheart*!' he muttered thickly, his breath ragged and uneven as she felt his strong hands ripping open her shirt, her flesh quivering at the touch of his tanned fingers on her bare skin. 'Lord knows what's happening to me . . . total folly . . . sheer madness!' he groaned incoherently, his lips sensually caressing the soft, full curves of her breasts.

'Madness . . .' she echoed helplessly, her mind groping confusedly after the sense of his words, and then, as his lips sought to possess first one hard, swollen peak and then the other, she moaned and cried out as her emotions spun completely out of control.

Possessed by an overwhelming surge of feverish excitement, she ran her hands over his strong shoulders, savouring the contours of his long body and the warmth of his skin beneath the thin cotton shirt before her fingers moved on down over his lean hips. He suddenly tensed at her touch, a deep growl breaking from his throat before his lovemaking became more urgent, more arousing, as his hands and mouth moved erotically over her body. Panting for release from the tension which seemed to fill her whole existence, she knew that all she had ever wanted was to lie beneath him, the touch of his skin against hers, the warmth of his fingers moving tantalisingly over the soft skin of her inner thighs . . .

And then—quite shockingly and suddenly—he had rolled off her warm, yielding body, swearing violently under his breath as he scrambled quickly to his feet.

'I'm sorry, Oriel,' he grated breathlessly, his chest heaving as if he was fighting for air. 'I . . . I must be mad—totally insane!' he added, before turning abruptly on his heels and striding swiftly back towards the castle.

Oriel lay on the ground, her eyes closed against the hot sun beating down from above as she tried to think what on earth she was going to do. It was some time since Jake had stormed back into the old fortress. What on earth was wrong with her? She may have spent most of her life buried in an old university town, but Oxford was full of good-looking, clever and sophisticated men, some of whom had made it quite clear that they found her equally attractive and good-looking. So why hadn't she fallen for any of them? Why had she never felt before this nervous, trembling excitement which scorched through her body whenever Jake came near her, the irrational urge to run her fingers through his thick dark hair, or the way her bones seemed to melt beneath the force of his slow, warm smile?

Oriel gave a heavy sigh, turning restlessly over on to her stomach and staring blindly down at a small beetle making its slow, erratic progress through the long grass. Nothing about her relationship with Jake seemed to make any kind of sense. She had always been able to divide her life into neat, tidy compartments, but now she found herself baffled and confused by her extraordinarily wild, emotional response to the man who had so dominated her trip to Syria.

Really—it was all too ridiculous, she told herself firmly. Anyone would think that—*oh, no*! She couldn't . . . no, it simply wasn't possible. She couldn't be in love with the horrid man, could she?

She moaned and buried her face in her hands. To have fallen in love with Jake Emmerson—*of all people*. How could this be happening to her? It simply wasn't fair! Her brain dissolved into chaos for a moment, her mind refusing to accept the very obvious response that even just thinking about him produced in her body—her shaking, trembling limbs, and a heartbeat which seemed to be rapidly pounding out of control.

'I don't believe it—it can't be happening to me!' she groaned out loud, scrambling to her feet and blinking in the strong sunlight as she gazed across at the jagged mountain peaks in the far distance. The phrase 'the heart has its reasons' floated through her mind, and she practically ground her teeth with fury. Her heart might have its reasons—but her brain certainly found them *totally* unacceptable. She and Jake had absolutely nothing in common, for heaven's sake! She and the horrid man could hardly agree on any subject at all. Except that . . . well, he wasn't really all *that* horrid, of course. In fact, ever since they'd arrived here at the castle, she and Jake had been getting on very well together. But they certainly didn't seem to have anything on which to build a deep, lasting relationship. So, if she had now come to the reluctant conclusion that she was in love with Jake—well, she could only imagine that she must be in the midst of a complete mental breakdown!

Oriel began pacing up and down over the grass, almost wringing her hands in agitation as she tried to find a solution to what must be—*pray God*—a brief, short-lived attack of wild infatuation.

OK. Calm down—there's no need to panic! she told herself firmly, trying to control the raging turmoil which seemed to have invaded her mind and body, as she began to gather up the sacks which they had earlier filled with cut grass. She could remember an American student once telling her, 'nothing propincts like propinquity'—and that was undoubtedly the cause of her present trouble. She and Jake had been thrown together, in a completely unnatural situation, miles away from any other living soul. He, having nothing else to do, had merely given in to a passing whim when he had kissed her so passionately just now. Oriel paused for a moment, unwilling to listen to the small, quiet voice inside her head which was reminding her that this was not the first time that she had been kissed by Jake.

'I don't regard that as significant,' she retorted out loud as she began to make her way towards the castle, dragging the sacks behind her.

Oh, no? But surely you have ended up in his arms every single time you've met, haven't you? the voice persisted. But Oriel refused to listen. Quite apart from anything else, Jake's mad dash back to the castle just now had clearly demonstrated that he, too, had no wish to become further involved. All she had to do, Oriel told herself, taking a deep and resolute breath, was to make sure that she didn't spend too much time alone with Jake. With any luck, the completely mad temporary infatuation which seemed to have struck her like a thunderbolt would hopefully burn itself out, without any further damage to what appeared to be her very susceptible heart.

Oriel had been so deeply immersed in her thoughts, it was only as she began to enter the

entrance to the castle that she realised she had
walked unknowingly across the small, thin
bridge over the fearsome ravine. A real case of
mind over matter, she thought wryly, before
becoming aware of a loud thumping noise as
she approached the arch which led into the
courtyard.

With his back towards her, stripped to the
waist and with his trousers rolled up to his
knees, Jake was busily engaged in chopping up
wood with the axe which they had found in the
museum.

Standing still within the dark recesses of the
arch, Oriel couldn't seem to tear her eyes away
from the smooth, rhythmic motions of his tall,
well-built body. Her stomach clenched as she
gazed at his broad shoulders and the strong,
rippling muscles beneath his deeply tanned
skin, feeling almost faint at the longing to be
held, once again, within those firm, brown arms.

Closing her eyes for a moment, Oriel took a
deep, shuddering breath and desperately tried
to pull herself together. With what seemed to be
an enormous effort, she eventually managed to
force herself to walk quickly and silently around
the edge of the courtyard, disappearing into the
dark recess of the large keep without attracting
his attention. By the time she had dragged the
sacks up the narrow stone staircase, she was
feeling totally exhausted.

You're in a bad way! she told herself,
disgusted to find that she had unconsciously

drifted over to the window to gaze longingly down at the figure far below in the courtyard. There was only one thing for it—she must try to cool herself down. And a quick dip in the ice-cold water of the reservoir seemed to be the ideal solution.

Jake raised his arms, bringing the axe down on to the rough log of wood before him. Goodness knows how many years it was since he'd been to summer camp with the rest of his friends from school. However, it was good to know that the skills he had learned there were now proving to be so useful. And that was just about the *only* good thing in this whole damnable situation, he told himself, raising the axe above his head once more before neatly cleaving the log in two.

The discovery of the axe had been a godsend. It was definitely helping him to release some of the strain and tension of the past twenty-four hours. Although being stuck here in this grim old castle, miles away from civilisation, was the very *least* of his present problems, he reminded himself grimly. How could he have allowed himself to have become so involved with Oriel? He'd given up trying to account for his extraordinary behaviour out on the grassy plateau. Just as he had been similarly baffled, and thoroughly perplexed, by his response to the quite maddening girl each and every time they had encountered one another during his official tour of Syria. It was seven years since

Barbara had run off with that Latin-American lover of hers. And, ever since his divorce, he'd been *very* careful only to become romantically involved with highly sophisticated women—those who knew how to conduct a light-hearted, discreet love-affair, with absolutely no commitment on either side.

But Oriel was definitely not that sort of girl. And so why—with danger signs flashing, alarm bells ringing, and all his years of experience behind him—he should still be so insanely attracted to her, he had absolutely *no* idea!

There was only one rational explanation—he must be temporarily out of his mind. Here he was, a well-respected American banker, looked up to by others in his profession and generally regarded as a thoroughly sane, cautious and prudent man. And yet, right from the very beginning of his trip to this country, his behaviour had been remarkable for its total lack of all sanity, caution and prudence.

Jake savagely cut another log in half, his mouth tightening into a grim line of deep annoyance and self-disgust. How could a man of his age and experience have been so foolish? Leaving aside all false modesty, he had no doubt that there were hundreds of perfectly nice, suitable and thoroughly charming women who would be only too happy to attract his attention. So, why had he allowed himself to become entangled with quite the most *unsuitable* girl he'd ever had the misfortune to meet?

Oriel de Montfort—a perfect example of a walking disaster—had burst in upon his life like some wildly alarming, dangerous firecracker. Quite apart from her annoying habit of lecturing him, as though he were one of her students, he also found it extremely disconcerting to have no idea of what the crazy girl was going to say, or do, next.

He paused for a moment, his expression relaxing into a reluctant smile at the recollection of exactly how she had opened the door of the museum. The use of her credit card *had* been ingenious, and, without it, they would never have found this axe. And, yes, she certainly knew her subject—because without Oriel's knowledge of old castles and the medieval way of life it might have been some time—if ever—before they had found the life-saving reservoir of fresh water. He also had to admit that she was surprisingly practical, especially when it came to matters such as filling those sacks with grass, and providing herself with some clothing. He closed his eyes for a moment, striving not to recall the sight of her slim body and long legs in those *very* brief shorts.

All right, so he'd given in to temptation—but so would any other red-blooded male. He was only human, after all! However, he thought grimly, it was clearly time that he pulled himself together. He was going to be sensible—oh, yes, he most *definitely* was! He was going back to Boston to marry Marcia Lowell. And if he found it difficult, at the moment, to feel madly enthusiastic about the prospect of a peaceful, calm existence in his house on Beacon Hill with the very beautiful, if equally calm, Marcia—well, that was just too bad!

Gazing down at the few remaining logs, Jake shrugged his broad shoulders. It was plainly quite ridiculous to have allowed himself to become so disturbed and disorientated by Oriel's presence here, alone with him in the castle. He was obviously over-reacting to what was, in essence, a very minor problem. As for the unfortunate fact that he found the English girl overwhelmingly attractive—well, it only went to show that such a regrettable emotional response could affect even the most sane and sensible of men. Once he had finished chopping up the remaining logs, he would go and have a swim in the cold, icy water of the reservoir. And, having thus banished any remaining heat in his body, he fully intended to make *very* sure that he would, in future, remain completely impervious to the alarming seductive charms of Miss de Montfort.

CHAPTER SEVEN

ORIEL squeezed out the last remaining drops of water from the pair of jade-green shorts. Finding that scrap of travel soap in a deep corner of her handbag had been a real piece of luck! She simply hadn't been able to resist the opportunity to scrub all the dust and sand from her clothes. But, unfortunately, she now found that, by washing everything, she had left herself with absolutely nothing to wear. It didn't really matter, of course, since her clothes would soon dry out in the hot sun. Luckily, Jake was fully occupied chopping up those logs of wood—and she simply couldn't resist the perfect opportunity to cool down her hot, sticky body. With a quick grin down at her pale, naked form, Oriel took a deep breath and dived into the enticing cold water of the lower pool.

Wow—the water really was freezing! However, swimming rapidly up and down the pool, she gradually became more used to the chilly temperature. So, this was what was meant by 'skinny-dipping'. She had never swum in the nude before, and was amazed at the wonderful feeling of freedom and relaxation engendered by the touch of cold water against her heated skin.

Turning over to float on her back, she gazed up at the high vaulted roof arching away above her. It was really rather spooky in here, the high, arrow-slit windows only allowing a small amount of cold, pale light to penetrate the cavernous darkness of the pool. She shivered, the goose-pimples on her skin reminding her that she had probably stayed in the water quite long enough, and she ought to get out now before she caught a chill.

Flipping back on to her stomach, she swam briskly to the far edge of the pool, where she had left Jake's brand new evening dress-shirt. He was probably going to be annoyed to find that she had helped herself to one of his few remaining pieces of clothing. But that was just too bad. It had been the only half-way decent garment which was guaranteed to cover her body—from neck to knee. All Halim's shirts were completely useless, being far too short—and, since she had just washed her only pair of underclothes, also thoroughly immodest. Goodness knows, she certainly didn't need *that* sort of exposure while she waited for her own clothes to dry out in the sun!

Struggling to get herself out of the pool, Oriel realised that she now faced a major problem. Why on earth hadn't it occurred to her that, while it was easy enough to jump down into the water, it was likely to be extremely hard to get out of it? She couldn't seem to get a foothold anywhere on the smooth, slippery mosaic-lined walls of the pool. And with the level of the water at least two feet lower than the stone edge above, she was fast coming to the conclusion that she had been not only careless, but a complete idiot. The more she struggled, the harder it seemed for the aching muscles in her arms to provide the necessary leverage to raise herself from the water.

'You look as though you need some help.'

Almost startled out of her wits by the sound of the deep voice echoing around the dark, chilly walls of the reservoir, Oriel looked up to see Jake bending down and extending his arm towards her.

'Grab hold of my hand, and we'll soon have you out of there.'

'But, I can't!' she wailed, shivering with cold. 'I . . . well, the fact is—I'm not wearing anything.'

'Don't be so damned stupid!' he exclaimed impatiently.

'All right . . .' she muttered, her teeth chattering together like castanets. 'But you've got to promise to close your eyes.'

'Oh, for heaven's sake!' Jake growled with exasperation, before quickly seizing hold of her wrist and dragging her slim, naked body from the icy cold water.

'*Ouch*! That hurt!' Oriel yelled, moaning as she bent down to rub her grazed shins, which had been scraped against the coarse, jagged stone at the edge of the pool. 'There was no need to be so rough,' she grumbled.

'There was every need,' he informed her
bluntly. 'The water in this pool is practically at
freezing point, for heaven's sake. How you could
have been so foolish, and——'

'Stop nagging!' she snapped.

'I wasn't doing anything of the sort!'

'Oh, yes, you were,' she retorted aggressively,
noting a muscle beating in his clenched jaw and
a dark flush spreading over his cheekbones as
he stared silently down at her in the dim light.
'If there's one thing I *really* can't stand, it's men
who . . .' She faltered, suddenly realising to her
complete and utter consternation, that she
wasn't just standing here cold and dripping
wet—*she was also stark, staring naked*!

Giving a strangled cry, Oriel swiftly turned to
pick up the shirt which she had left by the edge
of the pool. With her back towards him, she
feverishly tried to push her soaking wet,
trembling arms into the sleeves of the finely
woven silk shirt. But, however much she
struggled, the beastly material kept sticking to
her wet skin. She was practically swearing with
frustration when she felt a pair of heavy,
masculine hands on her shoulder, and Jake
quickly and efficiently helped her to don the
garment.

'You seem to have purloined my shirt,' he
drawled, turning her around and brushing aside
her nervous, fumbling fingers as he folded the
long sleeves back on her arms and then began
to fasten the buttons down the front of the shirt.

'Yes, I—er—I hope you don't mind,' she muttered, all the fight and aggression draining out of her as she quickly closed her eyes, trying not to tremble at the brief touch of his hands on her body as he did up the last button.

'Right, now let's get you out of here before you catch your death of cold,' he said harshly, a tense, strained expression on his face as he took hold of her arm.

'What about my clothes?' she cried, trying to wriggle out from beneath his tight grip and pointing towards the small pile of wet garments.

'You can see to them later. The first priority is to get you out of here and upstairs in the warm, where you can dry off.' And, taking no notice of her protests, he marched her out of the reservoir and along the dark passage, towards the huge space which had once housed the crusaders' horses.

'*Oooh!* Ow!' Oriel exclaimed, gingerly trying to avoid the small, sharp stones lying on the rough floor. 'It's all very well for you,' she grumbled, staring down at his long bare feet, which seemed to have no trouble coping with the stony surface. 'But it's very unreasonable to expect me—*aagh!*'

Gasping as she suddenly found herself swept up into his arms, Oriel took a moment or two to find her voice. 'Hey—what do you think you're doing?' she demanded breathlessly.

'Protecting your lily-white feet,' he drawled with cold mockery. 'Although I'm sorely tempted to wring your neck,' he added as she began to struggle wildly in his arms. 'And, if you don't quit wriggling, I'll throw you right back into that freezing cold water!'

'OK—OK!' she muttered, quickly realising that she was behaving in a thoroughly childish manner. Jake was merely being kind, and trying to prevent her feet from being cut to ribbons.

'Are you all right?' he asked, pausing for a moment on the threshold of one of the store-rooms to stare down at the silent girl in his arms.

'Yes, I'm fine . . .' she breathed huskily as she relaxed against the warm, bare skin of his broad shoulder. She felt extraordinarily faint and weightless, her senses bemused by the proximity of his tanned cheek only inches away from her own face, the dark lock of hair which had fallen over his wide brow, and the tantalisingly musky, masculine scent of his skin which teased her nostrils. As he entered the lower room of the keep and began to mount the narrow spiral staircase, she couldn't prevent a small sigh of contentment from escaping her lips, quickly lowering her eyelashes as he turned his head towards her.

'Oh, Oriel!' he mocked softly, his lips twisting into a rueful grin. 'What on earth am I going to do with you, hmm?'

'I don't know,' she murmured, snuggling closer to his broad, bare chest as he continued up the steep staircase, the unexpected warmth and amusement in his voice leaving her feeling weak and breathless. And then, impelled by some force beyond her control, she added softly, 'What . . . what do you want to do with me?'

Jake gave a harsh bark of laughter as he carried her into the large room on the upper floor of the keep. 'That's a damn stupid question,' he said, walking over to set her down beside the fireplace. 'You, my dear girl, must be blind, deaf and dumb if you don't know *exactly* what I want to do with you.'

'Must I . . .?' she whispered, swaying dizzily as she found herself on her own two feet once more.

'For heaven's sake!' he muttered under his breath, trying not to look at the delectable and revealing sight of his thin silk shirt clinging to her damp body like a second skin. And he certainly didn't need all those alarm bells ringing in his head to know that—if he didn't get himself out of this room in the next sixty seconds—he was going to be in deep, *dee-e-ep* trouble!

'Jake . . .?' she murmured helplessly as her legs began shaking uncontrollably. 'I . . . I don't know what's happening to me . . . but I feel most . . . most peculiar.'

'You're not the only one!' he breathed thickly, putting out a hand to support her trembling figure. Unfortunately, instead of clasping hold of her arm, as he had intended, he found his fingers closing about the full, warm curve of her breast.

Oriel quivered, her sharp intake of breath the only sound to disturb the sudden, still silence in the room. She was unable to move, unable to speak or tear her gaze away from the taut, strained expression on his face, the muscle beating frantically at the side of his clenched jaw, and the feverish glitter in his piercing grey eyes.

As the long silence deepened between them, they remained motionless, caught and imprisoned in a moment of time that appeared to be endless. It seemed as if there were no yesterday, today or tomorrow—only their two still figures trapped by some beguiling enchantment, bewitched and spellbound by an age-old force way beyond their control.

And then, very slowly, as if in a dream, or under some deep anaesthetic, he slowly and gently drew her closer to his tall figure. She could hardly breathe as she swayed helplessly towards him, her body trembling at the touch of his warm hands as they slipped beneath the thin, silky shirt. His fingers moved slowly upwards, tracing a scorching path over her bare, quivering flesh as he explored the slender curves of her slim hips and waist, before rising to gently caress the swollen fullness of her breasts, his fingers erotically tormenting their sensitive peaks.

Oriel gasped, a husky moan breaking from her throat at the tide of sensual delight flooding through her trembling body, clinging helplessly to his broad shoulders as her shaking legs threatened to collapse beneath her. 'Jake—I——'

He swiftly lowered his dark head—her words lost beneath the fierce possession of his lips as his arms closed about her, crushing her soft breasts against his hard chest and moulding her thighs against the long length of his body, so that she became sharply aware of his own arousal.

'I've been half out of my mind with wanting you . . .' he groaned against her mouth, before slowly raising his head and staring intently down into her sapphire-blue eyes.

The hoarse, deep, throaty rasp of his voice scarcely seemed to permeate her dazed senses. She felt as though she were possessed by a raging fever, and her body—which only a short time ago had been so icy cold—now seemed to be on fire, consumed by an overwhelming physical need that seemed almost beyond her control as she wound her arms about his neck, her trembling fingers burying themselves in his thick dark hair.

Barely a second later, she found herself being gently lowered down on to the pile of soft sacks filled with the grass they had gathered outside the castle. 'Sweetheart . . .?' he breathed urgently, kneeling down beside her and cupping her face with hands that shook with barely controlled tension. 'I guess this is just about my last, final moment of sanity. So, if you don't want to . . .'

'I *do* want . . . I want you to make love to me,' she whispered, her arms tightening about his neck as she pulled him down towards her, her lips parting breathlessly and eagerly, thirsting for his kiss.

A deep, responsive shudder vibrated through his long frame at her words, and he swiftly rolled over to trap her trembling body beneath him. Oriel's fingers clenched convulsively in the dark, thick texture of his hair as his mouth closed over hers with possessive, scorching intensity. She felt as though she was being swept along on a rushing tide of pure pleasure, her whole world encompassed by the sensual mastery of his lips and tongue as he savoured the inner softness of her mouth, nervous excitement spiralling through her veins at the pressure of his strong, muscular body pressed so closely to her own.

He gave a low groan as his lips left hers to trace a lingering path down the long line of her throat. And then, very slowly, as if savouring every moment, his hands moved to undo the buttons of the shirt, his fingers trembling slightly as he gently pushed aside the silky fabric to reveal the fine bones and soft, pale skin of her naked body, the burgeoning fullness of her breasts.

'Oh, how I've wanted to make love to you. Right from the very first moment we met,' he breathed huskily, his eyes darkening as he gazed down at her.

A fierce tide of excitement flowed through her at his words, her pulses racing at the dark flush beneath his tan as his eyes devoured the sight of her naked figure. As she gazed up at him, she was astounded to find that she felt not a trace of shame—only glorying in the fact that, if he thought her beautiful, then she *was* beautiful, every nerve and fibre of her body pulsatingly alive beneath the scorching gleam of his eyes.

A moment later he was swiftly stripping off his trousers, her blue eyes widening in appreciation of his hard masculine body as he removed and tossed away her silk shirt before lowering her gently back on to the comfortable, grass-filled hessian sacks.

'You're so . . . so incredibly lovely . . .' he whispered, his hands moving softly up over the warm curves of her thighs and waist to slowly caress her breasts, lowering his dark head to kiss first one swollen nipple and then another. Oriel gasped, moaning helplessly as his tongue erotically stroked their hard peaks. Tremors of delight shivered across her skin, her mind reeling out of control at the shafts of exquisite pain exploding deep in her stomach as he trailed his lips down over her body, sensually caressing and savouring the arousal of her flesh.

Racked and tormented by desire, her body writhed feverishly beneath him as the touch of his mouth and hands became more intimately sensual and demanding. She was on fire . . . unable

to bear another moment of such rapturous
torture. She could feel the blood pounding in
her head, and knew that she would either go
mad or die with the fierce, desperate need for
his physical possession.

His breath ragged and uneven, Jake stared
down at her for a moment as if to imprint on
his brain the soft, sweet curves of her breasts
and thighs. And then he gave a deep, husky
growl as he urgently parted her soft thighs. Oriel
cried out with ecstasy at the hard, powerful
thrusts of his body, a sweeping tide of such
storming intensity that she was sure she really
was dying—of delight and rapture. And as he
brought them both to the exquisite satisfaction
of mutual fulfilment, she shook and sobbed with
joy in his arms.

Oriel opened her eyes, blinking at the bright
shaft of afternoon sun streaming in through the
open, arched window. With a happy sigh of
contentment, she languorously stretched her
tired, aching body, a slight flush staining her
cheeks as erotic images of Jake's lovemaking
during the past few hours flooded through her
mind. No wonder she was aching! Her mouth
widened into a self-conscious grin as she
recalled not only Jake's seemingly insatiable
desire for her body, but the wanton
abandonment with which she had responded to
his sensual touch.

How could she have ever thought of him as

'stuffy'? A small, hysterical bubble of laughter fizzed through her body. He certainly had been remarkably *unstuffy* the two—or was it three?—times when he had aroused her from a lethargic, sleepy drowsiness, his passionate lovemaking almost instantly rekindling her own desire as he raised her to heights of sensual pleasure which she hadn't known existed. Even now, just thinking about the powerful thrusts of his long, lithe body, she could feel her stomach clenching with excitement.

Turning her head to look at Jake, who was lying fast asleep beside her, she gazed at the lock of dark hair lying over his handsome, tanned face, suddenly breathless as her heart skipped a beat, the world dizzily turning on its axis for a moment as a deep shaft of love seemed to pierce her soul.

Deciding not to wake him, Oriel carefully eased herself up off the soft, hessian sacks, slipping back into Jake's silk shirt before making her way down to the reservoir. Returning back up the spiral staircase some minutes later, she was carrying not only a selection of fruit and salad, but also the small pile of washing which she had done earlier in the day. Moving quietly, she placed the food down on the Minister's battered suitcase, and went over to explore a shadowy arch in a far corner of the large room.

Oh, of course! She should have realised that there must be access to the roof of the keep—a

perfect spot from which to keep a look-out over
the surrounding countryside, and just the place
to dry her clothes. A moment later she was
making her way up a narrow, steep staircase,
emerging on to a smooth, flat surface which was
protected by a three-foot high wall.

Busy spreading out her clothes on the hot
stone roof, Oriel gradually became aware of the
far, distant sound of an engine. Going over to
the edge of the tower, she gazed down at the
valley far below. Yes—it looked as if a truck was
making its way slowly along a winding road cut
through the far mountain range. Shielding her
eyes, she peered through the hazy sunlight.
Unfortunately, it was still a very long way away,
and she had no idea how to attract its attention.
And then, running to pick up the damp shirt
she had been wearing the day before, she was
just about to raise her arms, intending to wave
the shirt in the air, when she suddenly paused.
Thinking about it afterwards, she was never
quite sure what had prompted her to take
another, hard look at the vehicle as it drew
nearer to the castle. But her first, euphoric
excitement at the thought of their rescue quickly
turned to mind-numbing fright. She realised,
just in the nick of time, that the grey truck was
the very same vehicle which—only twenty-four
hours ago—had been used by Laila and her
terrorist friends to kidnap the Minister and
transport him off to captivity in Beirut!

'Wake up, Jake!' Oriel shouted, leaping down

the steep stone steps and dashing into the upper room of the keep.

'Umm . . .?' Jake murmured, opening his eyes and giving her a brief, sleepy smile before turning over and burying his face in the soft, hay-filled mattress beneath him.

'For heaven's sake—this is no time to go back to sleep!' she yelled, running over and kneeling down beside him. Putting her hands on the back of his broad shoulders, she shook his long, tanned body. 'Come on . . . wake up!'

With a heavy sigh of contentment, he rolled slowly over on to his back. 'What a wonderful girl you are,' he muttered happily, raising his arms and clasping her tightly to his bare chest. 'I'm not sure if I've got any energy left, sweetheart, but I'm certainly willing to try, and——'

'For goodness' sake!' Oriel giggled, momentarily distracted as he rolled her over on to her back, the descent of his firm mouth on hers preventing her from saying anything more for a few moments.

It was only when his lips slowly abandoned hers to move down her throat, towards the soft swell of her breasts, that she managed to pull herself together.

'No! Please, Jake . . .' she cried as she felt her body responding to his intimate touch. 'This isn't why I woke you up—you idiot!' she gasped. 'We're in serious trouble.'

'Hmm . . .?'

'We must do something, quickly. And I don't
mean that! she added with a slightly hysterical
laugh, trying to wriggle out from beneath him,
and frantically slapping at the hands now
intimately caressing her body. 'The baddies are
coming!'

'The *who* . . .?'

'Oh, you know,' she panted, finally managing
to scramble to her feet. 'Those terrorist friends
of Laila's. I'm almost certain that it's their grey
truck that I've just seen, on the far side of that
mountain range.'

Jake sat up, grunting as he brushed a hand
over his chin. 'I'd give a million dollars for some
soap and a razor,' he muttered.

'Your lack of any shaving equipment is the
very *least* of our problems at the moment. What
on earth are we going to do? It won't be long
before the terrorists get here—and then we'll
really be in the soup.'

'OK. Calm down. We're not going to get
anywhere by panicking,' Jake told her, rising to
his feet. 'How long before they get here?'

Oriel frowned and hesitated for a moment.
'I'm not sure.' She shrugged. 'It's difficult to
judge distances from up here. We might have
about an hour, I suppose. Although it could be
less.'

'And you're absolutely sure it's the same
truck?' he asked, walking over to the window
and staring across at the far range of mountains.

Oriel nodded and gave a heavy sigh. 'Yes, I'm

almost one hundred per cent sure, unfortunately.'

Jake turned his head to stare at her intently for a moment. 'OK, if you're that certain, then I guess we'd better get our skates on.'

'I see what you mean about the great view from up here,' Jake said a few moments later as they stood on the roof of the keep, his eyes following her pointed finger to where, in the far distance, he could see a vehicle making slow progress along the mountain road.

'It *is* the truck that took Halim off to Beirut, isn't it?' Oriel asked, raising a hand to shield her eyes as she peered into the distance.

His lips tightened. 'Yup, that's the one,' he agreed. 'And, from the distance it's travelled since you first saw it, I reckon we've got maybe three quarters of an hour to decide what we're going to do. My first instinct, since we're sitting ducks in this castle, is to try and get the hell out of here! However, I don't think that idea is a winner—particularly since there's nowhere to hide.'

Oriel leaned out over the tower ramparts. Jake was right. Other than the heavy, man-sized boulders down by the road, there was nothing but rough scrub and grass on the mountainside.

She turned back to him with a puzzled frown. 'I've thought about what you said earlier, and I still don't understand why they're coming back here,' she said with a puzzled frown. 'Surely that bomb they left in the car was supposed to blow us up?'

'Well . . . I must admit that it occurred to me, yesterday, that maybe the bomb was only intended to destroy the limousine,' Jake told her quietly. 'As I told you, I reckon they've probably decided—provided I'm still alive, of course—that it's worth making the journey back here to kidnap me.' He shrugged and gave her a wry grin.

'Goodness—you must be *stinking* rich!' she exclaimed, her cheeks flushing with embarrassment as he gave a hoot of laughter.

'Well, I don't know about "stinking", but I guess I am rich,' he drawled, his lips twitching with amusement. 'I and my family have certainly got enough dollars and cents to interest Laila and her friends.'

'Well, they're not going to get hold of you,' she said fiercely, throwing her arms about him for a moment. 'Not if I've got anything to do with it, they aren't.'

Jake held her tightly, burying his face in her cloud of blonde hair for a moment. 'I appreciate your sentiments, sweetheart, but I think we've both got to face the fact that we haven't much hope of evading the bad guys.'

'Oh, yes, we have!' she cried. 'We'll be quite safe, if we can just . . .'

The rest of her words were drowned in a mighty roar as a jet fighter, appearing from nowhere, suddenly swept over their heads, and just as suddenly disappeared, leaving only a trail of grey smoke behind.

'What on earth . . .?' Oriel gasped as two more jets, moving at the same speed and at the same frighteningly low level, flashed across their heads.

'The Syrian Air Force,' Jake muttered, shielding his eyes as he stared up into the sun.

'They must be looking for us!' Oriel yelled excitedly. 'You and the Minister were supposed to be at that oil installation, at Baniyás, yesterday—weren't you? So the balloon must have gone up when you didn't arrive, right?'

'Not necessarily.' Jake shrugged his broad shoulders. 'I'd like to believe the Seventh Cavalry were on their way—but I'm not sure I'd put any money on it.'

'Oh, for heaven's sake—don't be so defeatist,' she retorted. 'I don't know much about America, but, in Britain, our Government would take a dim view if the Home Secretary or the Minister of State for Trade and Industry were kidnapped by terrorists.'

Jake gave a snort of grim laughter. 'You can take it from me that "a dim view" is a considerable *understatement* of how the Government of the United States would regard such an act!'

'Well, there you are. As soon as the Syrians realised that you and the Minister had disappeared off the face of the earth, they'd have pulled in the Army, the police, and goodness knows who else,' she declared excitedly. 'And, since they're obviously looking for us, we've got to try and hold out here, until they come to our rescue.'

'Oh, sure . . .' Jake murmured sardonically. 'There's only one small problem—how do we do it? I don't see Laila, or her bunch of desperados, taking much notice when I lean over the ramparts and tell them not to come into the castle because the Syrian Army are going to be coming up over the hill any minute.'

'*For goodness' sake*! Haven't you been listening to a thing I've said over the last two days?' Oriel demanded, almost dancing with frustration. 'I've been telling you, *ad nauseam*, that you've got to stop thinking "twentieth century". If, over six hundred years ago, some crusaders were trapped in this castle, and they saw the fiendish Saracens coming up over the mountain—*what would they do*?' she asked with barely controlled impatience.

Jake shrugged, and then decided to humour the crazy girl. 'Well, I guess—' He hesitated. 'I guess they'd raise the drawbridge, and then lower the portcullis.'

'Very good! Go to the top of the class!' She gave him a mocking smile. 'So why don't we do just that?' 'Yes,' she added quickly as he opened his mouth to say something. 'I know that we can't do much about the bridge—but I don't see why we can't have a go at lowering that old portcullis.'

'And how are you proposing that we should

do that?' he asked, his voice heavy with scepticism.

'It's held up with chains, right? Now, I know they must be old and rusty, so why don't we try and break the links in the chains, either by smashing them with the axe, or by using the crowbar you took from the burnt-out remains of the limousine?'

Jake shook his head and cast his eyes up to heaven for a moment. 'I've got to hand it to you, Oriel—it's *such* a stupid, crazy idea that it may well work!' He laughed and glanced down at his watch. 'We haven't much time. So, the sooner we get down there and see what we can do with that rusty old portcullis, the better.'

CHAPTER EIGHT

ORIEL stood back to admire her handiwork, and then bent forward to push the end of the oil drum a little further over the wide, gaping hole in the ramparts above the entrance to the castle. Both she and Jake had been frantically busy over the past half-hour, and, now that they had almost finished their preparations for the defence of the castle, it was something of an anticlimax to find no sight or sound of either the terrorists or their grey truck.

Bearing in mind Jake's advice to keep herself as inconspicuous as possible, Oriel stood up and went to peer carefully over the edge of the ramparts. The mid-afternoon sun was blazing down and, apart from wishing that she had some cream to protect her fair skin from the heat of the sun's rays, Oriel would have given everything she possessed for a good pair of binoculars. Had she been wrong? Was it possible that she had mistaken some sort of mirage for the grey truck? She wasn't looking forward to the arrival of the terrorists, but neither was she looking forward to having to face Jake's wrath if, after all his hard work, it turned out that she had been hallucinating. But then, he had seen it too, hadn't he?

Oriel turned, leaning her back against the rough, warm stone as she gazed up at the keep, which towered above the rest of the castle on the far side of the courtyard. From where she stood, she could just see the upper half of Jake's tall figure moving around on the roof as he placed more wood on the fire. It had been a really brilliant idea of his to burn the old rubber tyre which they had found in the museum. He had warned her that it wasn't easy to set a mass of heavy rubber alight, but he had assembled a pile of wood on the roof and managed to get the tyre burning, its black smoke rising in a thick column up into the sky, visible for many hundreds of miles. She'd been full of praise for such an inspired idea, and also for his suggestion of using the remains of the heavily congealed white paint which they had found in the museum.

Following his directions, and using a small, flat piece of wood as a brush, she had managed to paint a large SOS across the floor of the open courtyard. In fact, once he'd got over his initial cynicism about her proposal to defend the castle against Laila and her gang, Jake had come up with some really great ideas. And, although he'd clearly doubted their ability to lower the portcullis, he had certainly attacked the chain with determination and gusto. It was only when he had abandoned the crowbar, and almost given up his attempt to smash some of the weakest links with the axe, that she'd heard his

shout of triumph—quickly followed by a
rumbling, thunderous sound as the heavy
grating had come crashing down across the
entrance to the castle.

'Don't get too excited, because it won't take
much of an effort to break through this old
portcullis,' Jake had warned her, after a close
examination of the thin metal bars which had
almost been eaten away by rust. But she'd
refused to allow him to dampen her spirits,
especially since she had a second line of defence
in mind. However, it had taken her quite some
time to persuade Jake to carry the oil drum,
which they had found in the museum, up on to
the ramparts.

'You're not *seriously* intending to pour boiling
oil down through that hole?' he had exclaimed
with horror. And her assurance that the oil
drum only contained a small amount of petrol,
and that, in any case, she had no method of
heating it up, had failed to set his mind at rest.
As she had explained, it was only *if* and *when*
they appeared to be in dire danger that she
intended to pull out the bung and let the petrol
trickle down into the passage below. Once she
had managed to set the petrol alight, it
would—with any luck—frighten the terrorists
and send them scampering back over the bridge,
and thus stop them entering the castle.

Quite honestly, as far as she was concerned,
it was a really *great* idea, and she'd been
somewhat annoyed when Jake had continued to

shake his head, muttering under his breath something like 'crazy females . . . bloodthirsty girl . . . blow us up to kingdom come!'

All of which, she now told herself, was totally ridiculous. With only a tiny amount of what he called 'gasoline', she was hardly likely to produce more than a very small fire, which would soon burn itself out. Besides—— She looked up as a shout from Jake interrupted her thoughts, and she saw him beckoning to her from the top of the keep.

'I can't think where that grey truck has got to,' Oriel said as she ran up the last few steps on to the roof to join Jake. 'I'm even beginning to wonder if it was a mirage.'

He shook his head. 'No, I caught a brief glimpse of it again just now. I reckon it will be with us in about twenty minutes.' He walked over to the edge of the ramparts, staring out into the distance. 'Since it's an old truck, it may have overheated trying to climb some of those mountains.'

'Pooh . . . what a smell!' she exclaimed, wrinkling her nose at the strong, acrid smell of burning rubber.

'It's all in a good cause,' he replied cheerfully, stoking up the flames beneath the tyre.

'So—what do we do while we're waiting?' she asked, suddenly feeling nervous and apprehensive now that there were no more preparations to make, or plans with which to keep her mind busy.

Jake glanced down at his watch. 'If we're going to try and hold Laila's gang off until nightfall, then I guess we'd better eat while we've got the chance.' And, although Oriel didn't see how she could possibly face any food, she had to agree that what Jake said made sense.

'Are you sure you don't want anything else?' Jake asked some time later.

'Oh, no, I honestly couldn't manage to eat another thing.' She gave him a rueful smile. 'After all that salad, I've got a distinct feeling that I'm about to turn into a rabbit at any moment!'

Jake laughed, getting up to go and put yet more wood on the fire before coming back to sit down beside her.

'I know it sounds silly to say so—but, if the terrorists *are* coming, I do wish they'd hurry up and get here,' Oriel muttered nervously.

'They say that waiting around is the toughest part of any action,' he agreed, placing his arm about her waist and drawing her closer to him. 'In fact——' He broke off, quickly sitting up and frowning for a moment before he jumped to his feet.

'Yes, I thought I heard an engine,' he said as she scrambled to her feet and followed him to the edge of the rampart.

Gazing down on to the road far below, Oriel saw that he was quite right. There, with a cloud of white steam issuing from the vehicle, was the battered grey truck which had been used to take

Halim off to captivity in Beirut. Grateful for the comfort of Jake's arm as he silently drew her close to him, Oriel watched the truck come to a halt in the small lay-by beside the blackened remains of the limousine.

'What do we do now?' she whispered.

Jake gave a bark of wry laughter. 'You don't have to keep your voice down, because they can't possibly hear what we're saying,' he told her, staring down at the men climbing out of the truck.

'But what *are* we going to do?'

He shrugged. 'You're the expert in medieval warfare, sweetheart. However, like the old crusaders, we've barricaded ourselves inside this castle, so I guess the next move is up to them.'

'Well, I wondered if it was any good trying to talk to Laila?' Oriel suggested. 'I know she's a thoroughly evil girl, but——'

'I *knew* there was something bothering me!' Jake clicked his fingers with annoyance. 'Where *is* Laila? She's obviously the brains of the outfit, but she doesn't seem to be with those men. So, maybe we don't have too much to worry about.'

Oriel's eyes narrowed as she stared down intently at the scene below them. Then she gave a sigh, turning to Jake as she said, 'We're out of luck. I expected her to be wearing a dress and high-heeled shoes, but I think that's her by the truck, shaking that man's arm and pointing up here, towards us.'

'You're right,' Jake said grimly. Now that they

were coming closer, he could see that Laila and her three male companions were clothed in the same dusty combat outfits printed with a camouflage pattern. And there was no doubt who was boss of the outfit. Screaming and shouting at the men, Laila was driving them upwards towards the grassy plateau in front of the entrance to the castle.

'They certainly seem to have been through the mill,' Oriel muttered. 'In fact, it looks almost as if they've been in some sort of battle,' she added as Jake seized hold of her arm, quickly pulling her down behind the shelter of the ramparts.

'Sorry, sweetheart, but the bad guys are getting just a little too close for comfort, and I don't want to take any unnecessary risks. What were you saying?'

'Well, I know it doesn't sound likely, but I was wondering if the Syrian Government—who have an army in Beirut—have been searching for Halim? Maybe Laila and her friends have been, quite literally, in the wars?'

Jake shrugged. 'It's possible, I suppose. However, if they've come back to collect me because I'm the only card they've got left in the pack, then they are likely to be *very* dangerous. So, I don't want you taking any unnecessary risks. OK?'

'OK, I've got the message,' Oriel said, trying to sound more confident than she felt. 'I may have written a book about medieval warfare, but I never realised that there's a whole world of difference between studying the subject and finding oneself actually taking part in a siege. Quite honestly,' she gave a nervous, shaky laugh, 'I think I've sort of *had* the subject, if you know what I mean?'

'I know *exactly* what you mean,' Jake said with feeling. 'And, from the shouts of rage outside the castle, it sounds to me as if Luscious Laila has discovered that we've lowered the portcullis.'

A moment later, there was a sudden *whoosh* as three jet fighters, flying in tight formation, swept past overhead and disappeared out of sight on the other side of the mountains.

'The Mounties to the rescue!' Oriel shouted excitedly, only restrained from jumping up and waving her arms by Jake's firm hand on her shoulder.

'Don't get too excited,' he warned her. 'They look impressive, but there's nowhere they can land here, is there? Frankly, sweetheart, what we need are some nice, heavy tanks to come rolling down that road to our rescue. And, until that happens, we've still got to deal with Laila, I'm afraid.'

'Well, Laila's in for a shock, isn't she?' Oriel said, trying to feel brave and confident as she gave Jake a nervous, trembling smile. 'She has yet to learn that our motto is "No Surrender"!'

'Oh, my darling,' he murmured, pulling her roughly into his arms and crushing her tightly to his chest for a moment. 'Everything's happened so fast, but I want you to know—whatever the outcome—that, for the first time in my life . . .' The rest of his words were drowned as the jet fighters swept over the castle once more.

'Oh, lumme! I'd better get down to the gatehouse and see what's happening,' Oriel shouted when she could make herself heard over the noise of the planes' engines. Dashing back down the stairs of the keep and across the courtyard, she tried to quell her anger at the Syrian Air Force. She was sure—well, almost sure—that Jake had been going to say that he had fallen in love with her. And maybe that *was* what he had intended to say—if only those beastly planes hadn't made so much noise. However, she didn't have any more time to think about her relationship with Jake as, carefully and gingerly, she made her way up on to the ramparts over the entrance to the castle. Moving warily, looking through one of the narrow slits in the stonework, she forgot her fright and apprehension for a moment as she gazed down at the scene in front of the castle. Three armed men were standing in a group on the other side of the small, metal bridge. And, despite all Laila's shouts and threats, it very much looked as if they were as frightened as Oriel herself had been about crossing the deep ravine.

Crawling over to where she had left the oil drum poised over the large hole, she bit her lip with indecision. It was no good relying on all three of those terrorists being too frightened to cross over the bridge. Eventually one of them was going to find the courage to scamper over—and then what? Unfortunately, Jake had been right when he had said that the portcullis wouldn't stand up to much of a battering.

Bending over the large, square hole, she became aware some moments later that at least two of the gang had managed to force themselves over the ravine. And, from the sound of it, it wouldn't be long before they broke through the flimsy metal grating, which was all that lay between them and the capture of the castle. There was clearly not a moment to lose, and she pulled out the bung at the end of the oil drum, tilting it up slightly to allow the petrol to flow down through the hole to the passage below. Picking up the oily rag, which she had left ready earlier in the afternoon, she removed Jake's lighter from the pocket of her shorts, trying to control her trembling hands as she set the rag alight. When she was sure that it was burning well, she dropped the rag through the hole—down on to the ever-widening, dark pool of flammable liquid below.

Thinking about the episode later, Oriel was forced to the conclusion that Jake had been, as always, quite right. She really *shouldn't* have ignored his dire warnings about playing around with dangerous materials. She certainly hadn't expected the sudden roar as the petrol was set alight—and neither had she realised that the fire and heat would be drawn upwards, through the tunnel to where she was crouching. As the flames roared towards her, she quickly jumped back, tripping over the oil drum and dislodging it down through the hole on to the fire below. The next few seconds seemed to pass in a blur. With shocked, glazed eyes, she watched the two men racing back towards the bridge, ignoring Laila's shouts as they continued running on down the mountain towards the grey truck parked on the lay-by. And then there was a mighty explosion, the ramparts shaking violently as if there had been an earthquake. And the next thing Oriel knew, she was lying in Jake's arms and he was anxiously asking if she was all right.

'I . . . I'm fine . . .' she muttered, trying to pull her scattered wits together. 'What's happened?'

His broad shoulders shook with laughter. 'I'll tell you what's happened,' he said, helping her trembling figure to her feet. 'I swear I've never seen anything so funny in all my born days!' he added, wiping the tears of laughter from his eyes as he pointed down to the grey truck. Rapidly accelerating away from the lay-by, it was being hotly pursued by Laila and one of the terrorists, shouting and waving their hands as they tried to catch up with the vehicle, which clearly had no intention of stopping.

'And that's not all—you crazy girl!' Jake added, gasping with almost hysterical laughter as he drew her to the edge of the ramparts. 'You'd better hope and pray that we get rescued soon. Because you didn't just set fire to that can of gasoline, and frighten off Laila and the bad guys—you've also managed to blow up the bridge over the ravine!'

Oriel gazed out of the window, groaning out loud as she saw that her normal view of the River Cherwell was, yet again, obscured by a torrential downpour. Would it never stop raining? Foreigners accused the British of being obsessed by the weather—but who could blame the inhabitants of this damp, wet island? In the two months since she had returned from Syria, it seemed as though there had only been one or two days of sunshine; the rest of the time it had been a case of heavy, overcast skies, or an everlasting deluge of rain.

Still, why should she care? she asked herself gloomily. The dull grey skies exactly reflected her dull grey life. Even the lecture she was due to give later this morning seemed to her to be unspeakably boring. Only a very keen student of medieval history was going to brave this sort of weather, just to listen to her on the subject of 'Kingdoms and Strongholds of the Crusaders'. And, even if anyone did turn up, the whole subject of her lecture was one which she would prefer to forget. Ever since she had inadvertently blown up the small metal bridge over the ravine outside Saladin's castle, her whole life had been going rapidly downhill.

It hadn't seemed like that at the time, of

course. She and Jake had been so thankful to have seen the last of Laila and her gang that they had been practically delirious with excitement and laughter. After a brief, refreshing dip in the icy cold water of the reservoir, they had made their way back upstairs to the keep, the dramatic events of the day leaving them both feeling tired and exhausted.

It had been Jake's idea to take the sacks of soft hay up on to the roof, where they had sat with their backs against the rough stone wall of the ramparts, watching the fiery red ball of the setting sun as it slowly slipped down over the horizon. It had been an all too brief time of perfect peace and warm companionship; a time in which they had talked of very little, both happily content in each other's company as they had savoured the quiet stillness of the night. And later, lying locked in each other's arms in the soft darkness, they had both fallen into a deep, dreamless sleep.

And that was exactly how they had been found—the brilliant, incandescent light from the helicopter overhead shining down with cruel, stark clarity on the two naked figures, their limbs so closely entwined with one another.

Oriel shuddered at the recollection of what had been quite one of the most awful, horrifically embarrassing moments of her life. Even now, a good two months after the event, she could still feel sick, her cheeks flooding with colour as she recalled the sudden arrival of the Syrian Air Force helicopters—one of which had landed outside the castle on the grassy plateau, while the other hovered over the keep. It was surely the material from which nightmares were made. Both she and Jake had been deeply asleep—so exhausted by the trauma of the previous day that they hadn't heard the approach of the aircraft until it was hovering overhead. And even then it had taken her dazed, confused mind some considerable time to realise exactly what was happening.

Amid all the confusion of whirling rotor blades, the loudly amplified, noisy static of the pilot's radio communication with his air-base near Damascus, and, above all, the glaring searchlight beating down upon her nude figure, it was quite a few minutes before she'd managed to pull herself together. And then, with a strangled cry, she had leaped to her feet, diving down the old stone staircase into the room below. Feverishly scrambling into what garments she could find, she had swiftly grabbed her handbag and some clothes for Jake before forcing herself to return back up the stairs to the roof.

She didn't think she would ever forget the deep embarrassment on Jake's face, clearly mirrored by her own, as she handed him the shirt and trousers which he had been wearing on the day of Halim's kidnap. Even now, she couldn't help flinching at the memory of the sly, broad grins of the two Arab Air Force officers, as they shinned down the ropes hanging from the helicopter above. Quickly snatching the clothes from her hands, Jake had hurriedly dressed himself, and a few seconds later they had both been winched up into the aircraft.

Dazed by the speed of events, and unable to make herself heard over the noise of the helicopter, there had been no time or opportunity to speak to one another. Even when they had landed at a military airport near Damascus, Jake had been so swiftly and urgently hustled away that she'd been given no chance for even a few, brief words of farewell to the man with whom she had fallen so much in love.

The next twenty-four hours had been equally nightmarish. Although the Syrian authorities had done their best to provide her with adequate clothing, hotel accommodation and a seat on the first aeroplane leaving the country for Europe, they had refused to tell her anything about Jake. Despite her desperate entreaties, there had seemed to be a total, official government silence about the American banker. The only information she did manage to extract—from a careless remark made just before her plane left the airport—was that the Minister of the Interior was alive, well and resting at his house in Damascus. So, if nothing else, she did have the satisfaction of knowing that Halim Khaddour had been rescued from his captivity in Beirut.

But, from that day to this, she had received no word or message of any kind from Jake Winthrop Emmerson III.

With a heavy sigh, Oriel walked over to her desk. What a fool she was, she told herself as she collected together the notes for her lectures. Every passing day of the two long, tedious months which had elapsed since her return from Syria had only increased her hopeless love and longing for the man with whom she had shared both danger and the most ecstatically happy moments of her life. Despite telling herself that it was completely illogical to expect Jake to feel the same way—obviously such an attractive, experienced man would have regarded their lovemaking as nothing more than an enjoyable, pleasant episode in a busy life—she had continued to pray for a miracle.

How stupid can you get? she asked herself roughly, gathering up her books and preparing to leave the room. Instead of tormenting herself with such a hopeless, forlorn yearning for Jake, she ought to be on her knees, fervently thanking God that at least none of her acquaintances, here in Oxford, had any notion of just what an idiot she had been. No idea of the few, brief hours of total madness in which she had acted so completely out of character and made such an utter fool of herself.

The rain was still bucketing down as Oriel cycled over Magdalen Bridge, swearing under her breath as she found herself drenched by a heavy spray of water from a passing car. 'It *really* isn't my day!' she muttered under her breath as she found herself being hailed by the portly, imperious figure of an elderly professor. With as much patience as she could muster, she stood waiting in the pouring rain while he tried to remember what it was that he had wanted to say.

'Ah, yes . . .' he wheezed. 'Do please give my regards to your dear aunt when she returns from her trip abroad, hmm?'

Eventually escaping, with the excuse that she would be late for her lecture, Oriel peddled furiously past the Botanic Gardens and on her way up the High Street to the Examination Schools, trying not to dread the return of her Aunt Harriet from her fact-finding visit to Angola.

She could only hope and pray that her aunt's trip would *not* result in the usual flood of refugees, who always seemed to arrive at the large house on the Woodstock Road in the middle of the night, and with no money to support either themselves or their dependants. Oriel, herself, had been forced to take refuge in her rooms in college for the past six weeks, driven out of her childhood home by the strange individuals she kept finding sound asleep on her own bed, and the incredible noise from so many people, speaking so many different languages.

Although, maybe she would have done better to have stayed in the house—even if it had begun to resemble the tower of Babel, she thought, coming to a halt and hurrying inside the large building. In the quiet and peace of her rooms in college, there had been nothing to distract her . . . nothing to interrupt the lonely hours in which, time and again, her thoughts had returned to Jake.

If she had hoped that the passage of time, and burying herself in her work, would cure her of the intense longing for his presence, and the aching need for the caress of his hands on her body—she had been doomed to disappointment. The long, long nights had been especially hard to bear. So many times she had fallen into an exhausted sleep in the early hours of the morning, only to awake at dawn to find her cheeks still damp with tears.

Taking off her wet mackintosh, and making her way up the wide marble staircase, Oriel made a determined effort to clear her mind of everything but the lecture she was to give in a few minutes' time. Entering the huge room which, with its high ceiling and baroque decoration, seemed more suitable for use as a ballroom, she placed her notes on the podium and waited while the undergraduates stopped gossiping and took their seats on the chairs placed in front of her.

After a quick head count, she was quite pleased to see that at least fifteen undergraduates had been prepared to brave the weather. Like most of her fellow lecturers, she was always haunted by the fear that there would come a day when—since lectures weren't compulsory and so few students attended them—she would find that no one had bothered to turn up. However, since those present today had obviously made an effort to get here, she intended to try and make her talk as short and concise as possible.

Taking a deep breath, she began briskly, 'Good morning. I am intending to outline, today, the foundation of the kingdom of Jerusalem by Duke Godfrey and the Frankish arms, through to its reconquest by Saladin . . .'

My feet are frozen! I bet I'm going to catch a cold—and no wonder, with all the rain we've been having! Oriel thought gloomily, some fifteen minutes later as she turned over a page of notes before resuming her lecture.

'With the accession of Baldwin II, the kingdom of Jerusalem reached its zenith. However . . .' She paused as the door at the far end of the room was thrown open with a loud bang. Looking up, Oriel suddenly stiffened, gasping as she stared with incredulous eyes at the tall man standing in the doorway.

CHAPTER NINE

SHAKING like a leaf, Oriel stood gazing with numb stupefaction at the tall, broad-shouldered man as he began walking slowly down the room towards her. Only the sound of his firm, measured footsteps disturbed the eerie silence in the large room. Even the undergraduates, after looking at her frozen face and body with some bewilderment, turned to watch his approach.

It wasn't until he came to a halt beside her that she began to start pulling her scattered wits together. Managing at last to open her mouth, she found that she could only make a hoarse, croaking sound, her vocal cords seemingly as paralysed as her mind. Clearing her throat, she tried again.

'J-Jake . . .? What . . . what are you doing here?' she whispered breathlessly, her knuckles white as she clutched hold of the podium to stop her shaking, trembling legs from giving way beneath her.

'That's a damn stupid question! I want to talk to you, of course,' he said, his deep voice echoing loudly around the room.

'But you *can't*! I mean, not here . . . not right now . . .' she gasped, continuing to cling on to the podium for support with one hand while she tried to push him away with the other.

'Want to bet on it?' Jake gave a harsh, sardonic laugh. 'I've been trying to get hold of you for the past six weeks, with a complete lack of success,' he said, catching hold of her hand. 'So, I'm sorry, sweetheart . . . but here I am, and here I stay, until we've got one or two things sorted out between us.'

'But . . . but you don't seem to understand—I . . . I'm in the middle of a lecture,' she muttered, desperately trying to tug her hand away from his grip, and only too well aware of the fact that her student audience was regarding the presence of Jake with considerable interest. His unexpected arrival was obviously providing an entertaining diversion from the usual dry as dust lecture.

'I want to know why you haven't replied to any of my letters, or returned any of my phone calls,' he demanded.

'I haven't had any letters or calls. And for heaven's sake—*keep your voice down*!' she hissed urgently, unable to prevent a deep tide of crimson from spreading over her face as she caught sight of the wide, broad grins on the faces of some of her students.

'We have to talk, and——'

'I can't *possibly* talk to you now—I've got to finish this lecture,' she wailed, still struggling to free her hand from his firm clasp.

Jake gave a loud snort of derision. 'I don't give

a damn about your lecture!' he thundered, his words drawing a muttered 'hear, hear' from one or two members of the audience.

'*Oh, lumme*! You're going to get me sacked!' she moaned. 'I . . . I'll talk to you later. But, please . . . *please*, go away,' she begged.

He stood looking down at her intently for a moment, and then turned to face the students. 'I'm sorry to interrupt your lecture, ladies and gentlemen,' he drawled smoothly. 'However, I hope you'll understand when I tell you that I'm a desperate man!' And, before Oriel had realised his intention, she found herself being pulled swiftly into his arms.

'*Jake*!' she gasped, but anything else she might have said was stifled as his mouth possessed hers with hard determination. Struggling against the arms which tightened about her like bands of steel, she was aware of a treacherous warmth invading her limbs beneath the kiss that burned and demanded her submission.

Gradually and imperceptibly, the ruthless pressure eased, his lips becoming warm and persuasive as they softly coaxed and teased away all resistance. Her heart was thudding; her pulse seemed to be racing out of control as her slim figure shook and trembled against his broad chest. She was lost, drowning beneath a sudden tidal wave of desire—totally unable to prevent herself from passionately responding to the sensual mastery of his tongue as he savoured the inner sweetness of her mouth.

Goodness knows where it would have all ended! But, while it took some time for her to become aware of the commotion surrounding them, Jake slowly raised his dark head and gave her a warm, tender smile as the noisy whistles and catcalls echoed around the large room.

'Well?'

'Hmm . . .?' Oriel stared up at his tall figure. Completely dazed and breathless, the only clear, concise thought in her head was that of gratitude for the hard strength of his arm about her waist. Without that support, she knew that her trembling, shaking legs would have given way beneath her.

'I reckon that, the sooner we get married, the better—don't you?'

Oriel caught her breath. '*What* . . .?' she gasped, quite unable to believe her ears. 'What . . . what did you say . . .?'

'I love you, and I'm asking you to marry me, Oriel,' Jake said firmly, the surrounding noise dying away amid various cries of 'Hush!' and 'Oh, do shut up!' from the more romantically inclined female undergraduates as they waited to hear what Dr de Montfort was going to say.

Dr de Montfort wasn't capable of saying anything! Well, not anything sensible, that was. For one thing, her brain didn't seem to be functioning at all, while her body was still throbbing and quivering from the devastating force of Jake's kiss. Had he really asked her to . . .? No—of course he hadn't. It was just some mad hallucination. She was going to wake up in a moment, and then . . .

Jake's mouth twisted into a wry smile. 'Come on, sweetheart—don't give me a hard time. Will you marry me? Yes, or no?' he added in an unsteady voice.

'This is crazy! I can't possibly . . . I mean, the whole idea is simply . . . it wouldn't work!' she cried helplessly.

'Yes, or no, Oriel?' Jake demanded harshly. His expression had become hard and forceful, his eyes glittering with an intense determination that seemed to drain her of any will-power.

'If you don't want him—I'll have him!' a pretty, red-haired student called out, her offer prompting further whistles and ribald comments.

Oriel's cheeks burned with embarrassment. The man was completely impossible. What on earth could she possibly say? She must have time to think . . . to consider . . .

'Oriel, you crazy, *maddening* girl!' he roared, giving her a furious shake. 'I want an answer—*right now.*'

'Oh, for heaven's sake! Yes . . . yes, I'll marry you,' she told him breathlessly. 'Now, will you please go away?'

'Oh, no!' Jake gave a triumphant laugh. 'OK, kids—class dismissed. That's it for today,' he added, giving the undergraduate audience such a warm, happy smile that it caused permanent damage to one girl's heart, and prompted another to shout, 'If she changes her mind—my name's Susie Harrison, and I'm at Balliol.'

'Thanks for the offer—if she gives me any trouble, I'll be right back!' Jake laughed over his shoulder as he grabbed Oriel's mackintosh and hurried her dazed figure from the room.

'This is quite ridiculous!' Oriel protested as he led her down the marble staircase.

'What about my bicycle?' she cried, as she was pushed into a large, chauffeur-driven Rolls-Royce.

'I'll have you know that kidnapping is a felony,' she declared as they were driven swiftly through the town.

'I'm definitely not going in there!' Oriel muttered as the limousine came to a halt outside the Randolph Hotel. 'And just *what* do you think you're doing . . .?' she demanded as Jake closed the door of his suite of rooms and took her firmly into his arms.

His shoulders shook with laughter. 'I intend to strip off your clothes—before making mad, passionate love to you for the rest of the day!' he said, removing her raincoat and undoing the zip of her dress as he propelled her across the carpet towards the bedroom. 'Any more objections?' he added, sweeping her up in his arms and placing her tenderly down on the huge double bed.

'Oh, no—none at all!' she sighed with a deep, ecstatic happiness as he clasped her tightly in his arms, the warm touch of his lips everything she had hungered for during the past, wretchedly unhappy weeks. 'Darling . . .?' she murmured breathlessly as he rapidly removed her last scrap of clothing. 'You haven't yet told me how you got out of Syria, or——'

'Not now—we'll talk about that later,' he said firmly, his powerful frame shaking as she undid the last button of his shirt and he felt her hands moving over the curly dark hair on his broad chest.

'Much . . . *much* later!' he breathed huskily before his lips claimed hers, igniting a raging flame deep inside her so that she rapidly lost all sense of time and space. The only reality was the hard warmth of his tanned body, the quivering ecstasy of his sensual, intimate touch and the erotic excitement that he was always able to invoke in her, as he brought them both to an earth-shattering climax in a storm of overwhelming passion.

'All right—I can see that the Syrian Government was probably embarrassed by the kidnapping of their Minister of the Interior; and I do understand that they kept quiet about *you*, for fear of an international row with the United States. But what I *don't* see,' Oriel added plaintively, blowing a soap bubble towards Jake, 'is why it took you so long to get in touch with me.'

'But I've already told you, back in the lecture hall, that I've been trying to contact you for the past six weeks.' Jake raised a bare foot to the tap, letting more hot water into the deep bath before turning off the tap with his toes. 'How's that?' he added.

'Hmm . . . perfect,' she murmured. 'However, I can assure you that I didn't get any letters or phone messages. In fact, there was nothing from you but total silence—from the moment the helicopter landed at that air-base near Damascus, until you turned up this morning,' she added sadly.

And, even now, she wasn't entirely one hundred per cent sure that she wasn't dreaming. So much had happened to her in Syria, both physically and emotionally, and in such a very short space of time. Was it really possible for her to be lying here, in the bath, alongside the man with whom she'd fallen so completely head-over-heels in love? The very same person whom she had regarded, initially, as one of the most detestable men she'd ever had the misfortune to meet? It simply didn't make any kind of logical sense!

'Have you *any* idea how many Turnbulls there are living in Oxford?' he demanded. 'Well, there's a hell of a lot—and I know, because I must have called every single one.'

'For heaven's sake.' She looked at him aghast. 'You didn't make all those phone calls from America, did you? It must have cost you *a fortune!*'

He grinned. 'Quite apart from the fact that I

am, as you once pointed out, "stinking rich"—I can assure you that I would have paid *anything* to track you down. And why not, when my whole life's happiness was at stake?'

'Oh, Jake.' She gazed mistily at him. 'How romantic!'

'Are you sure you don't mean "stuffy"?' he teased.

'Well . . .' She paused, trying not to smile, and gazing up at the ceiling as if in deep thought. 'Well, maybe . . . *aagh*!'

'Really!' Oriel giggled some moments later, her cheeks flushed as she struggled to sit up. 'That is positively the most *un*stuffy, and quite disgraceful behaviour I've ever come across!'

Jake laughed. 'You'd better get used to it, because I'm thoroughly enjoying my new image.'

'Oh, yes? Well, I think it would be improved by a *very* cold shower.'

'Oh, no—I've had enough of them to last me a lifetime. First in that damn castle in Syria, and then back home in Boston. I tell you, I was going frantic trying to get hold of you.' He sighed. 'And when I did eventually locate your house, I never did get to speak to you or your aunt. There was always some weird foreigner answering the phone every time I called, but I eventually got the message that your Aunt Harriet was still abroad. As for you—nobody knew where you were, except that you weren't sleeping at the house. And I can't begin to tell you how I felt about *that* piece of information.' He turned over in the water to look at her accusingly.

'Not guilty!' she said quickly. 'I couldn't take the bedlam from all those refugees, so I've been living a thoroughly puritanical, boring life in college for the past six weeks.'

'Oh, sure!' He gave a rumble of sardonic laughter. 'Anyone with such an amazing talent for not only causing mayhem and disaster, but who is also—at one and the same time—an extremely intelligent, warm and sexually exciting woman, must have blazed an unforgettable trail through the streets of this town. I simply don't believe you are capable of having a boring life.'

'Oh, yes, I am,' she assured him, secretly thrilled with the idea of herself as a scarlet woman. 'Unfortunately, I've never done anything at all interesting, or had any exciting adventures—not until my trip to Syria.' Her cheeks reddened as she raised her head and gave him a shy smile. 'And how could I possibly look at anyone else, when I was so much in love with you?'

'Ah, sweetheart!' he breathed softly, clasping her tightly in his arms and possessing her lips in a kiss of such piercing sweetness that she felt a sudden ridiculous urge to burst into tears. 'I became so desperate at not being able to fly over here and sort it all out. It took me some time, because you never told me the name of your college,' he added with a rueful shake of his head. 'However, I managed to track you down this morning—and the rest is history.'

'I imagine it must be, by now,' she agreed drily. 'I can't see any of those students keeping their mouths shut about the lecture this morning, can you? Especially not that dreadful girl, Susie Harrison,' she added grimly.

'Hah!' Jake gave a hoot of sardonic laughter. 'You're jealous.'

'No—I'm not!' she snapped, her cheeks flushing beneath his quizzical grin. 'I'm just worried about the gossip in my college—I bet I'm going to find myself well and truly on the carpet,' she told him glumly.

'Relax—there's no need for you to bother going back there. Other than to collect your passport, of course.'

'Don't be silly. Of course I'm going back.'

'No,' he said firmly. 'You're going to marry me—and, after a long honeymoon, we're going to be living in Rome.'

She sat up in the bath and looked at him with astonishment. 'We're *what*?'

'OK—let's take it from the top, shall we?' Jake said, getting out of the bath and putting on a towelling dressing-gown. 'You love me—right?'

'Yes, you know I do.'

'And you're going to marry me, so——'

'Now, hang on!' she said quickly, standing up as he held out a towel and wrapped it around her before lifting her out of the bath. 'It really won't work. I mean, we've nothing in common, and with my life here and your business in America——'

'I love you, Oriel—with all my heart,' he said simply. 'Nothing else matters beside that one, basic fact. I love you, and without you by my side life has no meaning. Besides, you promised to marry me in front of a whole lot of witnesses—and I'm holding you to that promise,' he added, his hands slipping inside her towel to slowly caress her trembling body.

'Oh, Jake—that's unfair . . .' she moaned helplessly.

He gave a soft laugh. 'Bankers aren't just rich—they're *re-eal* mean, too!' he murmured, picking her up and carrying her through to the bedroom. 'Now, sweetheart, I want you to listen to me for a moment—and then you can have your say, OK?'

'Yes, all right.'

He paused for a moment to collect his thoughts. 'I know we didn't have much time together in Syria—but I feel that I've lived through several lifetimes with you, even in such a very short space of time. And I know—with a total certainty—not only that I love you, but that I've never felt this way about anyone else.'

'Oh, Jake,' she murmured, her cheeks flushing with delight and happiness.

'Now, I've given the matter a good deal of thought,' he continued. 'In the beginning, I'll admit I was flummoxed, because our lives and life-styles are so very different. And then I started looking at the problem from a completely different angle, and I reckon I've got it licked. While I couldn't move my business to England, I was also sure that you wouldn't be keen to leave your academic life, here in Oxford. You could, of course, try and get a job at Radcliffe—which is one of the most famous universities for women in the States, and it's not too far from my home—but I decided the idea wasn't that great.' He paused for a moment. 'How about some champagne?'

'Wow—yes, please!' She grinned.

As he twisted the cork out of the bottle, Jake silently congratulated himself on his progress so far. There was no reason why Oriel wouldn't like Boston, and he was sure that she'd have been perfectly happy with the academic life at Radcliffe. However, after his mother's hysterics at the news that he had no intention of proposing marriage to Marcia Lowell, and intended to marry a young English girl instead, it had seemed a good idea to wait a few years before going back to live on Beacon Hill with his wife and, hopefully, a nursery full of children. He had never had any problem in handling his mother, but he wasn't prepared to have that elderly, imperious woman making his new wife unhappy in any way.

'By the way,' he said, placing a glass in her hands, 'how do you feel about us having kids? I've always hated the fact that I was an only child, and I reckon three or four would be just about right, hmm?'

'Well . . . I was terribly lonely at times, too,' she murmured. 'Although I think maybe two children would be fine to start with. A boy and a girl would be perfect!' She gave him a wide smile.

'I'm a lucky man!' he exclaimed, bending down to give her a passionate kiss. 'Right—where was I?' he muttered huskily, some moments later.

'Er . . . I think you had just discarded Oxford and Boston,' she said breathlessly. 'Although I'm still waiting to hear about Rome.'

'I want you to understand that, until my visit to Syria, I had been perfectly content with my life,' Jake said as he began to pace up and down the room. 'It wasn't until I met this crazy, absolutely maddening English girl that I realised what a boring existence I'd been living. And that, in the process, I'd also become extremely boring and——'

'Stuffy?'

He laughed. 'You're right! So, on my return to the States, I knew that I wanted to do something more interesting than just being a banker. Now, it so happens that I have a lot of contacts in the State Department, and, after our experience in Syria, I somehow seemed to be the flavour of the month. Also, I must admit that being "stinking rich" didn't hinder my prospects,' he added with a smile. 'So, after dropping a few broad hints, and generally making my desires known in the more influential corners of Capitol Hill, I can tell you that you're now looking at the new United States' Ambassador to Italy.'

'*Oh, lumme!*'

'I couldn't have put it better myself.' He grinned. 'There are a few hurdles before my appointment is confirmed, of course. I shall have to appear before a congressional committee, to have my appointment approved—and a fast language course in Italian seems a good idea—but, basically, that's about it. And, while I can guess that you might not be too thrilled about being the new ambassador's wife,' he added quickly as she opened her mouth, 'maybe you might like to think about the possibilities of Florence, or Venice.'

Oriel looked at him in confusion. 'I don't understand . . .?'

'You're into medieval history, right? And since you have finished writing your book about weapons and warfare—or whatever—it occurred to me that you might be a bit bored with crusader castles, one way and another.' He laughed as she groaned in agreement. 'So, how about the de Medicis—Lorenzo the Magnificent—Machiavelli and—er—a whole lot more I've forgotten?'

'Oh, Jake!' She giggled. 'You've been mugging up on Italian history!'

'I certainly have—and let me tell you that it's damn complicated! I reckon that it will keep you busy for a good long time. So, how about it, hmm?' he added, coming over to sit down on the bed beside her.

'Well . . .' She hesitated, but when she saw the uncertainty and tension in his face, she knew that she mustn't tease him any more. 'Darling Jake—I love you with all my heart!' she cried, winding her slim arms about his neck. 'I'd be happy and proud to marry you, even if you were out of work and we had to live in a shack. But I love the idea of Italy, and if you really think that I'm capable of being an ambassador's wife . . .?'

With a great shout of joy, he seized her in his arms, raining fervent kisses on her upturned face.

'For heaven's sake! We mustn't make too much noise,' she hissed, glancing at the small travel clock on his bedside table. 'Do you realise that it's *only* two o'clock in the afternoon?'

'How depraved can you get?' He grinned. 'However, as it's raining and there's nothing else to do, we might as well make the most of this comfortable bed, hmm?'

'Well, if you really can't think of anything else to do . . .?' she murmured, trembling as he slowly removed the towel from her slim figure, exposing her warm, creamy breasts, the tips swollen with desire.

'Absolutely nothing!' he assured her fervently, his voice dark with passion as he trailed his lips over her body. 'And since, at thirty-five, I'm not in the first flush of youth, I think we should force ourselves to practise the art of producing children, don't you?'

'Definitely!' she breathed, quivering as the hands caressing her became more pressing, more intimate.

'There's just one small item that maybe I should mention,' he murmured thickly. 'I think you ought to know that not only do twins run in my family—but that a distant cousin actually managed to produce triplets.'

'T-triplets . . .?' Oriel gasped as he moved to cover her with his body. *Oh, lumme!'*

Harlequin Presents®

Coming Next Month

#1351 ONE-WOMAN CRUSADE Emma Darcy
When Noah Seton takes over Toni's stepfather's company and dismisses twenty-seven people, Toni Braden decides to fight back. Everyone thinks she'll be no match for Noah—but they haven't counted on Toni's rather unorthodox ideas....

#1352 THE MUSIC OF LOVE Kay Gregory
Belinda truly doesn't mind that she's twenty-six and has never been kissed. Then Hal Blake jogs into her life and shows her just what she's been missing.

#1353 SO CLOSE AND NO CLOSER Penny Jordan
Rue decides to opt for the solitary life and is perfectly content—until Neil Saxton comes along. He's a demanding and dangerous man, so why does she miss him whenever he's not around?

#1354 INDISCRETION Anne Mather
Abby had loved Jake, but she'd lost him—and also Dominic, their child. Now Jake needs her. It's Abby's one chance to restore their relationship—if she can just find the strength to use the situation to her advantage.

#1355 BARGAIN WITH THE WIND Kathleen O'Brien
Darcy's only chance to save her business and her young sister from her lecherous stepfather's control is to get married—so she decides to accept Evan's repeated offer of marriage. But when she turns up in Florida, Miles Hawthorne, Evan's older brother, takes over the decision making!

#1356 AGAINST ALL ODDS Kay Thorpe
Brad Halston had pushed Kerry out of his personal life four years ago. Now he wants her out of his working life, too. But Kerry grew up during those years—and she isn't about to be pushed anywhere....

#1357 LORD OF MISRULE Sally Wentworth
Verity Mitchell simply planned to accompany her widowed friend, Paula, to meet Paula's in-laws in the country. Falling for Sebastian Kent is unexpected—and brings complications when Paula's life is threatened and Verity feels Sebastian is involved.

#1358 SHADOW ACROSS THE MOON Yvonne Whittal
Even after Anton de Ville tries valiantly to dispel Sarah's fears about marriage, she can't bring herself to accept his proposal. She loves him, but the misery of a past bad marriage makes Sarah wonder if she dares to love again....

Available in April wherever paperback books are sold, or through Harlequin Reader Service:

In the U.S.
P.O. Box 1397
Buffalo, N.Y.
14240-1397

In Canada
P.O. Box 603
Fort Erie, Ontario
L2A 5X3

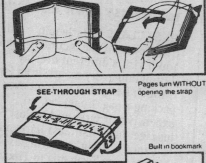